Clone

Also by Richard Cowper
in Pan Books

The Road to Corlay
Twilight of Briareus
Profundis

Clone

Richard Cowper

Pan Books
London and Sydney

First published 1972 by Victor Gollancz Ltd
This edition published 1981 by Pan Books Ltd,
Cavaye Place, London SW10 9PG
© Colin Murry 1972
ISBN 0 330 26179 7
Printed and bound by
Hunt Barnard Printing Ltd, Aylesbury, Bucks

for David and Annette

'Reason, in itself confounded,
Saw division grow together,
To themselves yet either neither,
Simple were so well compounded . . .'

SHAKESPEARE: *The Phoenix and the Turtle*

I

At 12.30 hours on September 3rd, 2072, Alvin had an eidetic hallucination. Since it was the first he had experienced the effect upon him was wholly unprecedented. He sat down on the stump of the Forsythe spruce he had just felled, clasped his hands across his chest and began to shiver uncontrollably.

Observing the lad's strange behaviour, his companion Norbert, a thirty-two-year-old *Antaen*-hybrid chimpanzee, switched off his laser trimmer and came over to see what was the matter. In the normal way Norbert was an ape of few words but he was extremely fond of Alvin and felt protective towards him. He rested his left hand on Alvin's right shoulder and gripped him reassuringly with his prosthetic thumb. 'You feeling all right, son?' he enquired.

By this time the severest of Alvin's tremors had abated a little. He swallowed manfully and blinked his eyes. 'I saw . . .' he began, and then shook his head.

Norbert peered round at the muddy ground all ribbed and churned with the imprint of their plastic boot soles. Alvin's saw was lying where he had dropped it. It had switched itself off. 'What about the saw?' he said.

Again Alvin shook his head. Unclasping one arm from his rib

cage he raised his hand and appeared to grope, somewhat hesitantly, at the empty air about eighteen inches in front of his nose. 'I saw this girl,' he said slowly, 'as real as you are, Norbert. I swear I did.'

Norbert frowned. Pushing back his helmet he scratched his deeply furrowed brow. ' "Girl"?' he repeated dubiously. 'What girl, son?'

'She had green eyes,' murmured Alvin dreamily, 'and dark brown hair.' He sighed. 'Oh she was as pretty as *myosoton aquaticum*, Norbert. Even prettier.'

The chimp realized that it was his duty to call up Control and report the matter, but something in Alvin's rapt expression restrained him. He consulted the timeteller strapped to his left wrist and said: 'We'll take our break now. You wait here and I'll go and fetch our packs from the buggy.'

He gave Alvin's shoulder a comforting squeeze, then knuckled his way crabwise across the slope and vanished among the trees by the water's edge.

All alone Alvin sat gazing out unseeing across the reservoir with an expression of near-idiotic bliss on his round, guileless face. Two large, happy tears gathered along his lower eyelids, brimmed over, and trickled unheeded down his chin.

Norbert returned five minutes later. He handed Alvin his lunch pack and sat down beside him on the trunk of the felled tree. 'I've been thinking,' he said. 'Maybe it was Doctor Somervell.'

'No, Norbert,' said Alvin firmly, 'I'm sure it wasn't anyone I've ever seen here.'

The chimp selected a sandwich from his own pack, peeled back a corner to expose the peanut butter filling, smacked his lips appreciatively and then took a healthy bite.

'Besides,' added Alvin reflectively, 'Doctor Somervell isn't pretty.'

'I wouldn't know,' said Norbert. 'She pinks up pretty good.'

'This girl,' said Alvin, ignoring the observation, 'had green eyes. Doctor Somervell has brown eyes.'

'Maybe she changed 'em,' shrugged Norbert, unscrewing the cap of his boiler flask and raising it to his lips.

'It *wasn't* Doctor Somervell,' insisted Alvin with some heat.

'After all, Norbert, I ought to know! I saw her!'

'No offence meant,' said Norbert wiping his lips with the back of his hand. 'Eat up, son.'

Alvin undid his pack, extracted an apple and took a moody bite out of it. For a minute or two he chewed away in thoughtful silence, then, swivelling round on his tree stump till he was facing the chimp he said: 'It could be from Before, couldn't it, Norbert?'

' "Before"?' echoed the chimp. 'Before what?'

'Before I was here.'

'There's no such thing,' said Norbert uneasily. 'You know that, Alvin. Hey, if you don't want that core, I'll have it.'

Alvin passed across the apple core and helped himself to a sandwich. He knew Norbert was speaking the truth simply because his earliest memory was of waking up in the Station's sick bay and seeing Doctor Somervell and Doctor Pfizier bending over him. That was when Doctor Pfizier had given him his name – 'Alvin'. Later, of course, he had acquired a whole host of other memories, but that was the first and it had always been Alvin's favourite. He found it quite impossible to express adequately either the gratitude he felt towards the good, grey-haired old Hydrologist who had introduced him to his identity, or the sense of almost dog-like devotion with which he recalled those early talks the two of them had had. 'Now you be good, Alvin,' the gentle old scientist had enjoined him, 'and let the others be the smart cookies.' How often Alvin's eyes had misted over as he recollected the fervent tremor in his own voice as he had replied: 'Oh, I *will*, sir! I *will*!' 'Blessed are the pure in heart, Alvin. Don't you ever forget that, my boy.' 'I won't, sir! Believe me!' 'Women are a snare and a delusion, Alvin.' 'Even Doctor Somervell, sir?' 'Mo's the worst of the lot, but don't say I told you.' The old man's wisdom had flowed like a pellucid, inexhaustible fountain and young Alvin had drunk deep.

If he had so far been unable to test the validity of many of the good doctor's precepts it was for the simple reason that adequate opportunity had never presented itself. Since the complement of the Aldbury Hydrological Station was restricted to Alvin, the two scientists and thirty-two prosthetized apes, the boy's temptations were minimal, and until the incident already des-scribed, he had not even felt anything that could be classed as

3

curiosity about his origins.

His cognizant life having been passed mainly in the company of the chimps, whom he had found to be in all significant respects immeasurably his superiors, Alvin felt none of the anti-anthropoid resentment that was still to be met in other less enlightened areas of the world. For their part, once the problem of his union membership had been sorted out, the apes accepted him in a brotherly way and had been happy to relieve him of the contents of his slender wage packet whenever he sat in on one of their Saturday poker schools. Eventually Norbert had felt constrained to call a branch meeting – from which Alvin had been tactfully excluded – and had told his fellow apes that it was a shame to take advantage of such a nice guy. Since then Alvin's regular losses at the card table had diminished remarkably and, once or twice, much to his amazement and delight he had even won a small pot.

The Station on which Alvin worked was part of the vast complex of artificial freshwater lakes that had been created towards the end of the 20th century to supply he ever-increasing demands of the London Conurbation. Some hundreds of square miles of rich agricultural land had been inundated and more would undoubtedly have suffered the same fate had not a series of increasingly violent earthquakes finally persuaded the government of the day that the money spent on re-building devastated towns might be more advantageously invested in de-salination plants.

The Aldbury Station was responsible for Lake Tring and Lake Gaddesden together with that area of the Chilterns which constituted their catchment area. Its principal duties were to monitor erosion, nutrient salt balance and biological productivity. Among its peripheral concerns were re-afforestation, tree culling, maintenance of fish stocks, hire of pleasure craft and management of the two refreshment centres. These tasks were left entirely in the hands of the apes who had also, on their own initiative, organized a round-the-clock, summer rescue service.

It was Alvin's most dearly cherished ambition to become a helmsman of one of the two Skeeto rescue boats. In his daydreams he sped up and down the ten-mile stretch of Lake Tring, his tangerine-tinted Zyoprene wetsuit glittering like a goldfish as he swooped to rescue beautiful maidens from watery graves. Unfortunately an inherent inability to distinguish between port and starboard at moments of stress seemed likely to preclude him from ever realizing his ambition. Bosun, the grizzled old ape who was in charge of the rescue service, had given strict orders that Alvin was never to be allowed near the Skeetos unless he was accompanied by a fully qualified chimp.

Alvin did not allow himself to become despondent. By dint of assiduous coaching from Norbert he could now average five correct port and starboard calls out of every ten, which, as he was quick to point out, was already halfway there. Meanwhile he occupied his weekends in assisting the female chimps to run the refreshment centres or, from time to time, in puttering round the lakes in the Station's Platypus with Norbert to check on anglers' licences.

At the time of his eidetic hallucination Alvin had been at the Aldbury Station for three years and four months. Biologically speaking he was then exactly eighteen years and two months old. Five foot five inches tall, with straw coloured hair, protruberant, pale blue eyes and remarkable ears that stuck out like pink handles almost at right angles from the sides of his round head, he was not perhaps the most handsome of youths, but he possessed something far rarer than mere masculine good looks, namely a truly beautiful character. There was something so undeniably saintly about Alvin that even the apes were moved to wonder. He appeared to live only to please others and they had soon wearied of sending him off to fetch them left handed lasers and cans of spotted paint because he was so obviously upset at being unable to gratify their wishes. He would return forlorn, his periwinkle blue eyes large with unshed tears and confess his failure in such abject tones that their laughter died on their lips and they patted him on the shoulder and told him not to take it to heart. Since that was so obviously just where Alvin *did* take it and since the apes, by and large, were a kindly lot, the game soon lost its appeal, and many of them agreed in private with Norbert who gave it as his opinion that God had sent Alvin to them to make them all better apes and to awaken the essential apeishness which slumbered within them.

From this it will be immediately evident that Norbert himself was no run-of-the-lab. anthropoid but as much a unique individual in his own way as Alvin was in his. Early in life Norbert had

5

'caught religion' and thought the initial fever had burnt itself out he had never been the same since. He now believed that everything had been put on earth for some divinely inscrutable purpose and that to those who kept an open mind and gave due reflection this purpose would one day be made apparent. He had been quick to perceive how well Alvin fitted in to this theosophical system and had gone out of his way to assist the youth towards the realization of his true potential. The happiest moment of Norbert's life so far had been when Alvin had turned to him one day and said: 'Norbert, with you and Doctor Pfizier around I know I'll never need to worry.' At that instant Norbert had his Pisgah revelation. His life's purpose was to shelter Alvin from the rough buffeting of a hostile world until one day, hand in hand and side by side, they would enter the Promised Land.

Alvin's vision of the girl with green eyes had disturbed Norbert more deeply than he cared to admit to the lad. Later that afternoon, when they had returned to the Station, he made a point of seeking out Doctor Somervell and laying the problem before her. He felt obscurely that this was a case for a woman's intuition and he was greatly relieved when she said: 'I'm glad you've told me this, Norbert. It's high time young Alvin was put straight on a thing or two. Send him along to see me after supper. Oh, and tell him to have a shower first.'

Confident that he had acted in Alvin's best interests Norbert bowed and left the room.

2

AT 42 MAUREEN SOMERVELL possessed the sort of Junoesque physique which, a hundred years before, might have led to her being referred to in awed tones as 'all woman'. By profession she was an analytical chemist and, as such, in charge of the water analysis at Aldbury. Although the daily sampling of run-off and its subsequent assessment was an automatic process in the control of a computer, 'Mo' Somervell was renowned for what she herself liked to call 'getting back to basics'. In the summer months she could frequently be observed, clad in a scarlet bathing suit, her splendid hams sheathed in a pair of transparent waders, dipping around with a sampling funnel on the marshy edges of Lakes Tring and Gaddesden.

Bent low over her work she presented an impressive expanse of bare pink buttock to the world at large and to the male apes in particular. At such moments atavistic impulse tended to re-emerge from the depths of the anthropoid hypothalamus, elbow its way through the Zobian-cultured cortical tissue, and flaunt itself vividly in the anthropoid anatomy, while across the simian faces conflicting emotions of wonder, doubt and despair flitted like shadows.

In their private discussions the younger apes maintained that she must be doing it on purpose, but most of the older ones held that it was just a happy accident. It only remains to be said that none of the chimps ever overstepped the bounds of propriety and that Doctor Somervell was never short of volunteers to help carry her equipment when she set out on one of her summer forays.

Her own attitude towards the apes resembled that of a kindly but authoritarian primary school teacher towards her pupils. Although the average anthropoid I.Q. was in the upper 120s she could never quite bring herself to believe it. 'I like to think of them as children – happy children,' she once confessed to a visitor. 'I daresay that's a pretty old-fashioned approach but it seems to work very well in practice.'

Her relationship with Dimitri Pfizier was a different matter. She herself had once described it as 'like the waters of Lake Tring – basically stable but liable to seasonal variations'. The stable elements were her admiration for Dimitri's professional expertise, a thwarted maternal instinct and pure habit; the variables her need for something more sexually satisfying than her temperamental, ten-year-old, Mark 3 nutatory paramour, and her subconscious outrage at Dimitri's recently expressed preference for the companionship of Zinnia, a six-year-old chimp with an affected lisp and a penchant for embroidery.

A recent attempt to programme her paramour with a retro-spective approximation of Dimitri's physical co-ordinates had been grievously frustrated by the temperature moderator going on the blink at the critical moment and drastically reducing the degree of tumescence. By the time the anthropoid service engi-neer had diagnosed the fault and put it right she had temporarily lost interest in surrogation. Since then she had been looking around for some direct method of re-kindling Dimitri's waning fire. Norbert's news seemed to offer just the opportunity she had been waiting for.

When Alvin, fresh from his shower and wearing his best zip-suit, knocked on her door and obeyed her summons to come in, he was slightly taken aback to find that she was not wearing her customary white overalls but a sort of semi-transparent, fluffy, pink and white knee-length garment that made her look as though she was swaddled in candy-floss. Her feet were thrust into a pair of pink, sequin-dusted powder-puff slippers. These, as far as Alvin could tell, were all she *was* wearing.

He closed the door carefully behind him. 'Norbert told me you wished to see me, Doctor Somervell.'

She smiled at him and patted the pneumatic couch. 'That's right, Alvin. Come over here and sit beside me.'

Alvin moved forward obediently and took his place at her side.

'My, you smell good!' she observed, leaning over him, flexing her nostrils and inhaling deeply.

Alvin blinked. 'Do I, Doctor Somervell? I'm glad you like it.'

'I certainly do, Alvin. But let's drop the "Doctor Somervell", shall we? You know my name's "Maureen", don't you?'

'Yes, Doctor Somervell.'

Doctor Somervell chuckled tolerantly. 'Well, perhaps one thing at a time, eh? Now what's this old Norbert's been telling me about you and some girl or other?'

'Oh, *yes*, Doctor Somervell!' Alvin's moon face became luminous with reminiscence.

'Well, go on.'

Alvin clasped his hands in his lap and sighed. 'She had green eyes, Doctor Somervell – the colour of duck-weed – and peat brown hair – sort of short. She was looking down at me . . . and *smiling*. . . .' His voice tailed away and his own lips beamed in

8

reverie. He looked supremely idiotic and, at the same time, rather touching.

'Did she *say* anything to you?'

'Oh no, Doctor Somervell. She didn't need to.'

Doctor Somervell chewed her lower lip reflectively. 'Whereabouts was she?'

Alvin frowned. 'She didn't seem to be anywhere in particular. I mean not here or in the lake or anything. But I think she was sort of bending over me ... or something. ...'

'Not in bed?'

'No. I would have remembered that.'

'Who do *you* think she was, Alvin?'

Alvin looked uncomfortable. 'I – I don't know, Doctor Somervell.'

'Norbert said you'd suggested she might be from Before.'

Alvin coloured like a peony and began to scratch his head violently – a sure sign with him that he was being assailed by feelings of guilt. 'Oh, did I? I ... I ...'

'You know that's quite impossible, don't you, Alvin?'

Alvin nodded miserably.

'Then why did you say it?'

'Because I'm sinful?' he suggested feebly, but with a note of hopeful pleading.

'Not sinful, Alvin. *Weak*. Now tell me the truth. You made it all up, didn't you?'

'Did I, Doctor Somervell?'

'Of course you did. It's an obvious, immature, sexual fantasy.'

'Oh,' said Alvin dismally.

'You know what *that* is, don't you, Alvin?'

Alvin shook his head.

'Oh, come now, Alvin. Don't tell me you've never thought about girls.'

Alvin blushed again.

Doctor Somervell slid herself along the couch till she appeared about to overwhelm him like some vast pink blanc-mange. With one hand she turned his face towards hers and gazed speculatively into his eyes. 'You can tell *me*, Alvin,' she murmured, and the fingers of her other hand seemed to stumble by happy accident on the thigh-tab of his zip.

Alvin swallowed manfully. 'Girls?' he gurgled.

'Yes, *girls*, Alvin,' she throbbed. '*Women*, Alvin. *Us!*'

Her face loomed up over his so that he seemed to be peering straight up her flared nostrils. Their proximity induced in him a curious sensation of helplessness. He opened his mouth to make some pertinent observation but, before the words could material-ize, her lips had descended upon his and something, which for a wild moment he supposed to be her thumb, was frisking around inside his mouth like a chunk of indiarubber. Then a lot of rather unlikely things seemed to happen all at once. By the time he regained possession of his senses it was to find himself lying on his back on the couch with – incredibly! – Doctor Somervell squatting on top of him. What was going on beneath the volumi-nous folds of her pink négligée he could only guess at, but he was aware of a sense of insufferable, anguished yearning, of elation and despair and, all too soon, of rapidly impending crisis. 'Oh, Doctor Somervell!' he gasped. '*Oh . . . Doctor . . . S-o-m-e-r-v-e-l-l!!*' At which moment the door opened and in strolled Doctor Pfizier.

Instead of turning on his heel and retreating he nodded to them, sauntered across the room, and having subsided into a prehensile loafer, crossed one leg over the other, picked up a video-viewer and began squinting through it.

Alvin gazed up at Doctor Somervell and wondered what would happen next. He was conscious of no feelings of guilt since he reasoned that whatever had happened (was, indeed, still happen-ing!) had been at her express wish. He was therefore considerably surprised to hear her say: 'You ought to be thoroughly ashamed of yourself, Alvin. And I thought you were such a nice boy too!'

'Been misbehaving himself, has he?' enquired Doctor Pfizier, glancing up from his viewer. 'I must say I'm disappointed in you, Alvin.'

Alvin's blue eyes filled with tears. Censure from Doctor Pfizier was the unkindest cut of all.

'What's he been up to, Mó?'

Doctor Somervell rocked herself ruminatively backwards and forwards, thereby causing Alvin to bite his tongue. 'He asked me to demonstrate the technique of buccal resuscitation, Dimitri. Something to do with his rescue service tests, he said.'

'Crafty, crafty,' nodded Doctor Pfizier, uncrossing his legs and scratching his groin. 'And so?'

'And so, of course, I showed him.' She sounded so sincere that Alvin almost found himself believing her. 'And before I knew what was happening he was taking advantage of me.'

'Bad,' grunted Doctor Pfizier. 'Very underhand.'

'That's just what it was, Dimitri. Underhand.' Frowning abstractedly, Doctor Somervell slipped her own hand beneath her and gave Alvin a tweak that made his eyes pop like mushrooms.

'Well, Alvin,' said Doctor Pfizier, 'what have you got to say for yourself? Come on, lad. Speak up!'

'I'm very sorry, sir,' gulped Alvin. 'I didn't mean to do anything wrong. I thought –'

'You thought it was high time you found out whether Miss Somervell was as delectable a dish as I've always told you she was,' said Doctor Pfizier smacking his lips. 'Well, is she?'

'I – I don't know, sir. I mean –'

'Haven't you got anything to drink in this nunnery, Mo?' demanded Doctor Pfizier, cutting him short. 'I seem to recall–'

'In the cabinet, Dimitri. You might fix me one too, while you're at it.'

'Sure thing, doll.' Doctor Pfizier flung down the viewer and, clicking his fingers in a syncopated rhythm, skipped through into the adjoining room.

Doctor Somervell took advantage of his absence to prise herself free. 'Do fasten up that zip, Alvin,' she said. 'It really does you no credit.'

Alvin struggled up into a sitting position and adjusted his dress. He looked dazed and dejected. 'May I go now, Doctor Somervell?' he enquired tearfully.

'Do,' she said, 'and mind you close the door after you. There's a terrible draught from somewhere.'

3

At 11.30 the following morning Alvin was summoned to Doctor Pfizier's office. The Doctor, looking alert and purposeful, but a shade paler than when Alvin had last seen him, came straight to the point. 'What's this Mo's been telling me about you and some girl or other, Alvin?'

Alvin told him.

'Someone you've met around the lake, I suppose.'

'Oh, no, sir.'

'Well, we can't have you ramping around taking advantage of any stray female you happen to meet, Alvin. They aren't all as tolerant as Doctor Somervell, you know.'

'But I'd never seen this girl before, sir.'

'Is that supposed to make sense?'

'I don't know, sir,' said Alvin sadly.

'And that trick you pulled last night,' said Doctor Pfizier, switching his line of attack. 'Not very nice, was it?'

Alvin blinked. 'Nice, sir?' he queried vaguely.

'Haven't I always told you, Alvin? Once a lady always a lady! *Toujours la politesse.* Besides, Mo's old enough to be your mother.'

'Yes, sir.'

'So what are we going to do about it?'

'Sir?'

Doctor Pfizier took a thoughtful turn up and down the room. 'According to our records you're down as "null libido", Alvin. Do you know what that means?'

'No, sir.'

'Girls aren't supposed to interest you.'

Alvin's eyes opened even wider.

'That surprises you?'

'Well, yes, sir – I mean, no sir.'

'Tell it to Doctor Somervell, eh?'

'Sir?'

'So the records are wrong. Which means there's been a balls-up at the M.O.P. Not for the first time, I'd say.'

Alvin looked blank.

'I've tried to do my best by you, boy. God knows it hasn't been easy, but I've tried. Now I discover there's a fundamental flaw in the matrix. All my hard work gone for nothing. It's a bitter disappointment, I can tell you.'

Alvin began to weep silently.

'*Mens sana in corpore sano*,' muttered Doctor Pfizier. 'As the twig is bent so is the tree inclined.' He sighed hugely. 'Well, there's nothing else for it, I'm afraid. Back to square one.'

Alvin snuffled wetly and dragged his sleeve across his dripping nose.

'Oh, cheer up, lad,' said Doctor Pfizier. 'Your heart's in the right place. Maybe they'll send you back to us and we can start over again.'

'B-back, sir?' gulped Alvin.

Doctor Pfizier nodded optimistically. 'I don't see why not. Shouldn't be too difficult to sponge the slate clean. I'd take you along myself only I can't spare the time. I wonder who's due for a spot of furlough?' He skipped across the room and questioned a video cabinet. Three numbers appeared on the screen. Against one of them a point of light winked saucily. 'Twenty-seven,' said Doctor Pfizier. 'That's Norbert, isn't it?'

Alvin nodded.

'A thoroughly sound chimp our Norbert. You couldn't be in better hands. I'll call up the M.O.P. and let them know you're coming.'

Alvin sniffed deferentially. 'What is the M.O.P., sir?'

'Ministry of Procreation,' said Doctor Pfizier. 'Professor Poynter knows all about you.'

'Do I *have* to go, sir? Can't I have another chance?'

Doctor Pfizier stepped forward and put his arm round Alvin's quivering shoulders. 'But that's just what we're giving you, son. A few little adjustments and you'll be back here again in a couple of weeks as bright as a button. We can pick things up again right where we left off. That's what you want, isn't it?'

'Oh, *yes*, sir,' breathed Alvin fervently.

'Well then, you trot along and pack your grip while I put Norbert in the picture. You can catch the shuttle from Aylesbury and be down in Croydon before dark. Might even have a chance to see a bit of the big city. You'd like that, wouldn't you?'

'Would I, sir?'

'My goodness, yes!' enthused Doctor Pfizier. 'There's nothing like it! That's what civilization's all about, Alvin! Where it's all happening! Tremendously exciting!'

Alvin's face brightened a little. 'I wish you were coming too, sir.'

'So do I, Alvin. So do I. Maybe some other time. Now you'll want a bit of ready cash, I daresay. Are you due any wages?'

'Two months, sir.'

'Two months, eh? Well, collect it from Jefferson before you go. I'll have him make you out a travel warrant, too. And you'll need your identity card. You won't get far without that.' Doctor Pfizier slapped him on the shoulder and grinned encouragingly. 'You'll be all right, son. There's lots of good material in you. And just between the two of us, I daresay Mo wasn't altogether as innocent as she makes out. But we can't afford to take risks, can we? It's better this way. Scrap and start again. Profit from our mistakes, eh? That way we'll all be proud of you yet, Alvin. I'm convinced of it.'

But Alvin wasn't really listening. He was seeing the girl with green eyes again. She was smiling at him.

Doctor Pfizier, observing his expression of entranced imbecility, sighed and propelled him gently from the room.

4

ALTHOUGH BOTH ALVIN and Doctor Pfizier were wholly ignorant of the matter, the boy was in fact the brain-child (along with three identical brothers) of the aforementioned

Professor Miriam Poynter, O.B.E., D.Sc., F.R.S., P.L.S., F.Z.S., etc. She it was who, with her own two lips, had pipetted the long frozen sperm and introduced it to the chosen egg. She, and she alone, had observed with bated breath as it lashed its frenetic way into the zona pellucida and came at last to rest, all passion spent, with its weary little head flat on the surface of the vitellus. Forty-eight hours later, when the zygote was already busily dividing, hers was the finger which, at the critical moment, had touched the switch and administered one minute electric shock to the blastocyst which caused it to have second thoughts and induced the inner cell mass to split into two identical halves. Twelve hours later a second shock had induced a second division. Within a matter of days Alvin, Bruce, Colin and Desmond, as yet sexless and anonymous, were at last free to grow their separate ways, having been transferred, one by one, into four placentas which had once belonged to four large Berkshire sows. There in the cosy, uterine darkness, laved by synthetic placental fluids, the genes which carried the peculiar inheritance of Alvin's progenitors were able at last to transmit their mysterious messages unimpeded to their embryonic cells.

The reason why Sir Gordon Loveridge – Professor Poynter's immediate superior – had allowed her to embark on her genetic alchemy at a time when any form of artificially induced multiple conception was virtually a capital offence, lay in the unique qualities of the man and the woman who had produced the gametes. Both were eidetic freaks, blessed (or cursed) with the ability to remember everything that had ever impressed itself upon their insatiable neurones.

The father, a civil engineer, had succumbed to acute melancholia and passed away in the spring of 1983 at the age of 42. His ultimate mnemonic triumph had been to recall successfully the names of the individual members – together with those of the substitutes, the referee and the resulting score – of every team in every Association football match that had ever been played in the United Kingdom since 1887.

The mother, after working for fifty dull years in the Records Division of the Department of Inland Revenue, had now in the Indian Summer of her days found fame and fortune as the Resident Human Encyclopaedia of a Double-Your-Money

Sonar-Visonic Quiz Show. Such were her phenomenal powers of recall that she seemed certain to retain her crown until the day she cackled out her last useless fact and dropped dead under the studio lights.

The one fact of which she was totally unaware was that she had become *mater in absentia* of Alvin and his three brothers. When she had undergone a hysterectomy at the age of 34 it had not occurred to her that her extracted ovaries, tagged 'Eidetic Alpha (?)',would be dropped into the deep freezer vault at the Ministry of Procreation. There they had languished until some twenty years later, Professor Poynter had re-discovered them and had been inspired to thaw them back to life, extract a ripe egg and unite it in unholy matrimony with the posthumous ejaculate of Frederick Arthur Watkins 'Eidetic Alpha(?)'.

The experiment was a triumphant success. Alvin and his brothers came to full term, were delivered and, on March 3rd, 2054, drew their first outraged breaths in the experimental wing of the Croydon incubator unit. Due to the extremely delicate nature of the population crisis their advent had to be kept a closely guarded secret. As soon as it was practicable they were separated and handed over to four pairs of carefully selected foster parents, none of whom was informed that the infant they were cherishing was in fact a quadruplet.

By the time they reached the age of five it was becoming plain, at least to the initiated, that they had all inherited their parents' extraordinary gift. A series of tests, surreptitiously administered by Professor Poynter in the guise of a peripatetic Health Visitor, proved beyond doubt that Alvin, Bruce, Colin and Desmond were all equally incapable of forgetting absolutely anything whatsoever.

Apart from this there was nothing about them to distinguish them from a million other little boys. They were neither outstandingly bright nor remarkably dim, just average, and since neither of their parents had been blessed with exceptional good looks they did not earn the envy or enmity of their playfellows on that score. They were, however, virtually precluded from playing various childish games such as 'Pelmanism' and 'I remember: I remember' on the grounds that they didn't play fair. These accusations caused them a certain amount of puzzled heart-searching until they realized that it was almost as easy to pretend to forget as it was to remember. From that moment on they had no further social problems.

Professor Poynter maintained her contact with her brood and kept an up-to-date file on each one. They were all so extraordinarily alike that she sometimes found difficulty in remembering which was which and on more than one occasion she had earned herself a puzzled stare by addressing Desmond as Bruce, or Bruce as Colin –or was it Alvin? She had no very clear idea of where her research was leading her, or indeed, how her four clones might prove useful to society other than as perambulating memory banks, but she persuaded herself that something significant would emerge eventually. As it happened she was proved right, though hardly in a way which she could have foreseen.

Shortly after their fifteenth birthday Miriam Poynter entered the expressavator which whisked her up to Stratum 402 of the Crystal Palace Tower. She was keeping her biannual appointment with Bruce who lived in Module 115 with his foster parents the Robinsons and their elder daughter Fiona.

After having interviewed the clone to her satisfaction and re-assured herself that the onset of puberty had deprived him of none of his eidetic powers, Professor Poynter was just preparing to take her leave when the lad peered over her shoulder and announced solemnly: 'They're cutting open your belly and taking your tubes out, Miss Poynter.'

'Why, Bruce, what a very strange thing to say!'

'Well, they are, Miss,' he averred. 'And the man who's doing it's got red hair.'

'Red hair?' chuckled Professor Poynter. 'Well, well. Whatever next?' And with that she bade the Robinsons adieu and descended the two thirds of a mile to the ground.

Two days later she made a similar journey, this time to Stratum 344 of the Barbican Monument. Here she called upon young Colin who occupied Module 278 with *his* foster parents the MacDonalds and their sixteen-year-old son Robert. Professor Poynter noted for her record that, like Bruce, Colin's eidetic gift was unimpaired by his sexual development. She was, nevertheless, considerably taken aback when, at the end of the interview, the clone said: 'What are they operating on you for, Miss Poynter?'

'Operating on me? What *do* you mean, Colin?'

Colin's pale blue eyes were fixed on some point beyond the back of her head and, as she watched, she saw them move as though he were indeed observing something curious going on.

'He's opening you up right down the middle,' he said. 'Ugh!'

'But I'm here, Colin! Right in front of you! You're just imagining it.'

Her final words were addressed to the empty air. Colin, a sensitive lad, had turned pale and rushed out to the toilet.

By the time Professor Poynter got round to Alvin, the last of the four, she felt like an Australian aboriginal who has had the misfortune to find himself on the receiving end of a bone-pointing ritual. After Desmond, totally unprompted, had hallucinated the third version of the same grisly picture, only the obstinacy bred of a lifetime's scientific scepticism had prevented her from charging into the Hammersmith Hospital and demanding an immediate laparotomy. Now, as she finally confronted Alvin, she found that her fingers were trembling so violently that she all but dropped the case of stereoscopic mnemonic transparencies and fumbled badly as she fitted them into the viewer. Alvin, as helpful as ever, did his best to put her at her ease, though he was somewhat at a loss to understand why it was that Miss Poynter kept staring at him so intently and seemed to jump several inches into the air every time he opened his lips.

When eventually the tests were completed Alvin carefully replaced the slides in their case, closed the lid and pushed the container back across the table to her. She stared at him as though hypnotized. 'Was there something else, Miss Poynter?' he enquired politely.

Professor Poynter swallowed with some difficulty. 'I was wondering, Alvin, whether you were seeing anything *unusual*, today? About *me*, I mean?'

Alvin regarded her gravely, his round head tilted slightly to one side. 'Like what, Miss Poynter?'

The rational scientist in Professor Poynter rose and wagged an admonishing finger at her. 'Just – well, anything *unusual*, Alvin.'

The clone considered. 'You look quite a bit older than when I saw you last,' he said finally.

'Then you don't see anything else? Anything *behind* me, say?'

Alvin peered dutifully at the apartment wall behind her head. 'Well, only that man in white, with the sort of torch thing.'

Professor Poynter fainted.

Exactly three weeks later, supine in a private ward in University College Hospital, she pondered on what had happened. A neat pink scar stretching from her sternum to her pubic stubble offered incontrovertible proof that what the clones had foreseen had indeed come to pass. Coiled within her she now had 137 centimetres of brand-new, crash-cultured, laser-grafted intestine replacing the cancerous conglomerate which had been excised.

The surgery had been performed by Mr Daryl Ravenswood, an acknowledged master of this type of operation, and since Professor Poynter was every bit as distinguished in her own field as he was in his, he had made a special point of dropping in to see her the next day. Afterwards, discussing the interview with his mistress of the month he remarked: 'A peculiar old duck. Couldn't seem to get over the fact that I've got red hair.'

Sister Petunia Corbeille contemplated him pensively from beneath the thicket of her platinum eyelashes. 'And all over, too,' she murmured.

5

PROFESSOR POYNTER RETURNED to her duties some six weeks later, still undecided as to the correct explanation for what had occurred. As far as she could see there were only two possible solutions – pure coincidence, or some form of auto-suggestion. In order to bring the first of these into perspective she set about programming the M.O.P. computer to assess the mathematical odds against the coincidence, given that none of the four clones had knowledge of the others' existence. The data was sketchy and, admittedly, subjective, but even so the resultant trial of 'O's before the decimal point went a long way towards confirming her in her opinion that pure chance, though by no means impossible, was too unlikely to warrant further serious consideration.

That left her only auto-suggestion and here she found herself confronted by the familiar precedental paradox – had she developed the disease because they had told her she would, or had they told her she would because she had already developed the disease? Which came first: the carcinoma or its prognostication? The more she pondered the matter the further she seemed from finding a satisfactory answer. Allowing that the nature of the boys' descriptions of what they had seen was all of a piece with their customary methods of eidetic recall, how could they possibly have 'remembered' what had not yet taken place? Having reached that point, for the first time in sixteen years Miriam Poynter began seriously to wonder whether she had been wise to embark on the experiment in the first place.

Her decision to assemble the four adolescent clones and observe their reactions was not lightly taken and she was scrupulous in apprising Sir Gordon Loveridge of her intention. He was greatly intrigued by the idea and at once agreed to the proposal on condition that he would be allowed to witness the confrontation on closed circuit So-Vi. For reasons of security it was decided between them that the clones' own recollections of the actual meeting should afterwards be erased by a prudent whiff of azaguanine-12.

Accordingly, on July 1st, 2069, four electric buggies might have been observed jinking and threading their programmed way by four carefully chosen routes across the capillary network of the metropolis to converge, simultaneously, upon four separate entrances to the Ministry of Procreation. Out of them stepped Bruce, Colin, Desmond and Alvin.

Each sublimely ignorant of the others' existence, they were conducted individually to four pre-selected cubicles where they were instructed to sit down and watch the video-screen before them. A few moments later the screens flickered into 3-dimensional life and there was Miriam Poynter smiling reassuringly in upon them. Choosing her words with great care she refrained from addressing any of them by name as she explained in some detail the nature of their peculiar gift and what was known about it. Four pairs of identical blue eyes regarded her stereoscopic image solemnly as Alvin, Colin, Desmond and Bruce each absorbed the notion that he was a genetic freak.

Her address concluded, Professor Poynter faded from their view and, one by one, they were conducted along a corridor into the very room from which she had been addressing them.

Comfortably ensconced in his private sanctum on the 28th floor Sir Gordon watched the boys enter. Aesthetically they were not particularly prepossessing specimens he decided, and touched the control button which brought up the sound just in time for him to hear Professor Poynter saying: 'Then this must be Alvin.'

Alvin, the last to enter, looked doubtfully at Bruce and Desmond and Colin, and they looked just as doubtfully at him. As far as Sir Gordon could judge they appeared mildly astonished, but little more. Then with one accord they turned and stared owlishly at Professor Poynter. Four mouths opened simultaneously and from them all one perfectly phrased question emerged: *'Who are we, Miss Poynter?'*

It was not the easiest question Miriam Poynter had ever been called upon to answer but she did her best. She had just passed the point in the history of their genesis where, as embryos, they had been transferred to their surrogate placentas, when Sir Gordon saw the clones glance round at each other and then turn back to confront their maker. The next instant Professor Poynter's head had vanished from his screen and been replaced by that of a large pink pig! The four boys promptly collapsed into hysterical laughter. The pig-headed chimera, apparently unable to divine the cause of their mirth, paused in mid-sentence, whereupon its head was again removed and replaced in rapid succession by that of a chimpanzee, a rhinoceros, a polar bear and a St Bernard.

Sir Gordon was out of his chair and halfway across the room to the screen when Professor Poynter reappeared, still seemingly oblivious of what had been going on, looking exactly as she had always looked except that this time she was completely naked and, as far as Sir Gordon could judge, adorned with at least one extra pair of breasts. 'Extraordinary,' murmured the Senior Scientist of the M.O.P. retreating fascinated to his chair. 'Doesn't she *realize*?'

At this juncture some altercation seemed to develop among the clones. During the course of it Professor Poynter's auxiliary mammaries were twice removed and replaced. 'Boys! Boys!' Sir Gordon heard his Chief Geneticist plead: 'If only you'll give me a chance to explain –'

At which point she vanished completely.

Alvin, Bruce, Colin and Desmond regarded each other accusingly and said with one voice: 'It wasn't me!'

'One of us must have,' said Colin.

'Well, I didn't,' said Bruce.

'Nor did I,' said Alvin.

'Tits is one thing,' said Desmond pontifically, 'but rubbing the old girl out is sneaky. Anyway, who took mine off her?'

'I did,' said Bruce. 'You had them much too far down.'

'I didn't! Mine were the top lot!'

'*Mine* were the top lot!'

'You must have done it then!'

'I swear I didn't! Android honour!'

'Android honour!'

'Android honour!'

'Android honour!'

The question as to who was responsible for Professor Poynter's disappearance was still unsettled when the door burst open and in she stormed. Normally breasted, stark naked but for a gas mask, she clutched in her right hand a yellow plastic cylinder. Without pausing to explain what she was about she thrust her arm out before her and gave the surprised clones a full ten-second burst of atomized azaguanine-12. Then with an agonized glance towards the concealed camera, she fled.

'What a woman!' exclaimed Sir Gordon reverently. 'Protein for you, Miriam!'

By the time Professor Poynter, temporarily attired in a technician's smock, returned to the room and switched on the ventilation fans, the four clones were flopped out like so many mackerel with four identical smiles wreathed blissfully across their four moon-like faces. She probed briskly at their pulses then summoned in two anthropoid orderlies who stacked the unconscious boys on to a floater and guided it out.

Half an hour later and more appropriately clad, the Professor was lofted to the 28th floor.

'Amazing, Miriam!' opinioned Sir Gordon. 'Quite amazing! I wouldn't have missed that for worlds! Are you feeling all right now?'

Professor Poynter coloured brightly.

'What does it feel like being – well, do we call it "translated" or "teleported"?'

'You think that is what it was?'

'Don't *you*?'

'I find myself singularly unable to form any rational opinion whatsoever on the matter.'

'The young rascals,' chuckled Sir Gordon. 'On the whole I liked the St Bernard best.'

'I beg your pardon?'

Sir Gordon blinked. 'You don't remember?'

'Remember what?'

'The – ah – "chimeras"?'

'Did you say "chimeras"?'

'Then you didn't see them?'

'See what?'

'Nor the extra breasts?'

'I *beg* your pardon!'

'Amazing,' murmured Sir Gordon. 'Truly amazing.'

'Would you care to be a little more explicit?'

'Well, take a look at yourself, my dear.' So saying, Sir Gordon shuffled over to the video-screen console and set it for play-back. The screen pulsed into rapid motion as he sped back retrospectively through the interview to the point where the clones had gone into their huddle. 'Now,' he said. 'Watch this!' and adjusted the controls for normal viewing.

They gazed spell-bound as the 3-dimensional fantasies once more blossomed forth within the womb of the screen. When the performance was over the Professor turned to her chief, her eyes frantic with a wild surmise. 'But that must mean it actually *happened*!' she shuddered.

Sir Gordon permitted himself a discreet eyebrow shrug.

'Well, did it, or didn't it?' she pursued desperately.

'I confess that it does seem rather unlikely that the camera could have recorded a purely *subjective* hallucination,' he murmured apologetically.

'You mean you believe that I – *I actually became those monsters*?'

'Well, Miriam, since you press me, I must say that from where I'm standing it does begin to look rather like it.' Sir Gordon chuckled reminiscently. 'Typical schoolboy waggery, really. I'm surprised the young scamps didn't attempt something androgynous. How are they now, by the way?'

'Still out when I left,' observed Professor Poynter with an unmistakable undertone of grim satisfaction. 'I must have given them more A-12 than I'd intended. I admit I *was* in a bit of a wax.'

'Perfectly understandable,' nodded her chief. 'In your place I daresay I'd have been simply livid.'

'But what are we going to *do*, Gordon?'

Sir Gordon stroked his moustache ruminatively. 'Well, obviously we've got to keep 'em apart for the time being. Leastways until we discover exactly what it is you've cooked up there. I confess this strikes me as being one of those cases where the whole is likely to prove a great deal more puissant than just the sum of its parts. All things considered, perhaps it's just as well you settled for quads, eh?'

Professor Poynter shivered. 'You know, Gordon,' she said, 'for the first time in my life I think I know what Rutherford must have felt like when he discovered he'd split the atom.'

'Yes, indeed,' nodded Sir Gordon. 'And we all know what *that* led to, don't we?'

Two hours later the four clones opened their eyes to discover that they had no idea who they were, where they were, or what they were doing there. Apparently their memory proteins had all been bleached whiter than white. Unsmirched by the smudge of even a solitary recollection, the grey and glaucous cells stretched far away.

Professor Poynter had all along made the understandable but unfortunate error of assuming that their mnemonic circuitry operated in the normal way only more so. By the time she realized that theirs was different not in degree but in kind, the damage had been done. Four hastily arranged electro-encephalograms appeared to confirm her worst fears. Azaguanine-12 had done its work only too well. As individuals Alvin, Bruce, Colin and Desmond had been utterly and absolutely erased. In their places were four po-faced, adolescent anonymities.

24

'Not to worry,' said Sir Gordon blandly when, distraught and aghast she videophoned the news to him. 'It'll give us time to recoup. I'll toddle off and draft an official regret note to the foster p's and get the Minister to sign it. In the meantime we'd better board them out through "Personnel". They *are* still *compos mentis*, I take it?'

'Oh, yes. It's simply that they don't remember *anything*!'

'Just as well in the circumstances, eh?'

'But I feel such a *lemon*, Gordon.'

'Fret not, Miriam. The raw material's still there in the vaults, remember.'

'Yes, I suppose so.'

'And I'll see you get due credit in the next Hons. List.'

'You know it isn't *that*. . . .'

'Well, something anyway. Just you leave it to me.'

'You *are* a brick, Gordon.'

The 'something' which the prudent Sir Gordon settled for in the end was, in fact, an album of selected stereograph stills from the original video-recording. This he duly presented to Professor Poynter at a *tête-à-tête* dinner in his Regent's Park penthouse some six weeks later. It was to become one of her most dearly treasured possessions.

By that time Alvin and his brothers, ignorant as the dawn, purged, refined and psychologically reconstituted, were already industriously acquiring new identities for themselves in various odd nooks and corners of a grossly overpopulated globe.

6

THE LONDON SHUTTLE was two hours late at Aylesbury, its anthropoid driver having succumbed to a severe attack of residual G-bend intoxication shortly after leaving Birmingham. By an administrative oversight his co-driver happened to be a member of a rival union whose rules expressly forbade him to touch any control other than the emergency brake on odd days of the month. The automatic Network Pilot having been specifically programmed never to intervene in any inter-union dispute, promptly switched itself into neutral and went into temporary hibernation. The whole South-bound Inter-City Expressway system between Glasgow and London was thereby effectively paralysed for the 120 odd minutes it took to locate a replacement driver and ferry him out to the point of the breakdown.

Norbert and Alvin, ignorant of the hold-up, assumed that the shuttle which whined into Aylesbury at 1502 hours was the 1500 from Birmingham running, remarkably, only two minutes later. They were informed of the true situation by an irate passenger. Fixing Norbert with an ill-tempered eye as the chimp clambered into the compartment behind Alvin, he added gratuitously that it was high time he and his bloody hairy mates got their bloody plastic thumbs out and started doing an honest bloody day's work for their bloody living.

Curiously enough this was Alvin's first personal experience of anti-anthropoidism though he had often overheard the apes at Aldbury discussing it among themselves. Turning, he remarked that he was sure the gentleman would wish to know that Norbert had the reputation of being the hardest and most conscientious worker on the whole Aldbury Station.

The man's thick lip wrinkled in a sneer. 'You his boy friend or something, darling?'

'Of course I am,' said Alvin. 'Norbert and Doctor Pfizier are my two best friends in the whole world!'

'Another bloody monkey-lover! No wonder the country's on its bloody knees! You ginks are a bloody disgrace to the human race!'

Alvin was puzzled by this exchange and would gladly have prolonged the discussion had not Norbert drawn him forcibly away up the compartment and installed him in a seat well out of casual conversation range. Having placed their luggage and his hat on the overhead rack, the chimp sat down and showed Alvin how to secure his lap belt. Then he extracted a well-thumbed copy of Jeremy Taylor's *Holy Dying* from his pocket and settled down to read.

Alvin looked about him with interest. The seats, which were rather similar in design to those of a 20th Century jet air liner, were grouped in fours round small tables. Those opposite to his and Norbert's were occupied by two elderly ladies, one of whom now leant across and stage-whispered to Alvin: 'I think it was most commendable of you to speak up for your friend like that.'

Alvin blushed. 'Oh well,' he said, 'that gentleman wasn't being at all fair. After all, Norbert's our branch leader of the A.T.S.W.'

'Is he indeed? Did you hear that, Peggy?'

Norbert turned over a page and frowned.

'Doctor Pfizier says I couldn't be in better hands,' Alvin informed them. 'Norbert's taking me down to Croydon. Do you know Croydon?'

'Oh yes. We live in Wimbledon. It's very close. By the way, my name's Margaret.'

'Mine's Alvin.'

'Well, Alvin, and what are you and Norbert going to do in Croydon?'

'We're going to see Professor Poynter about my libido.'

A buzzer sounded in the compartment and, a moment later, the landscape had begun to drift murmurously away past the porthole. The woman named Peggy produced a round metal dish which she placed on the table before her. 'I think we still have time for another game, Margaret. I wonder if Alvin and his friend would care to join us?'

'Yes, *do*,' urged Margaret. 'It's *so* much more fun with more than two players.'

'All right,' said Alvin. 'How do you play?'

Peggy materialized five coloured dice from somewhere about her person, set the inner surface of the little dish revolving with a touch of her finger and dropped the dice on to it one by one. They skipped and hopped and finally came to rest. 'Twenty-one and two doubles,' she announced. 'I'll just try the odd one for a full house.'

She removed four of the dice from the dish on the table, set the inner surface revolving again and dropped in the remaining cube. When it came to rest she clicked her tongue in annoyance. '*Not* very good,' she said. 'Your turn, Margaret.'

Her companion collected up the dice and repeated the procedure. 'Oh dear, oh dear,' she sighed. 'Only eighteen and a miserable pair. I'm sure Alvin will beat that easily.'

Alvin did. He scored twenty-four and a triple five.

'Bravo!' applauded Margaret. 'And now Norbert.'

Norbert looked up from his book, blinked thoughtfully, and asked to be excused. The two ladies tried hard to persuade him but he remained politely adamant.

'Well, that's one to Alvin, then,' said Peggy and from her purse she extracted a £10 piece which she passed across to the clone. Margaret did likewise. Alvin protested but they both laughed and assured him they would soon win it back.

Alvin won the next game too. And the next. 'Oh, you're a lucky one and no mistake,' chuckled Margaret. 'No wonder Norbert wouldn't play with you.'

Norbert smiled a trifle grimly and said nothing.

But as the shuttle approached the outskirts of the city Alvin's luck began to change. His scores were still high but somehow theirs were just a little bit higher. Then he won again. At that point, on Peggy's suggestion, the stakes were raised to £20 a throw. Norbert cleared his throat and tried to catch Alvin's eye, but without success.

In no time at all it seemed, Alvin had parted with the first of his two months' pay and would, no doubt, have parted with the second also had not Norbert, in standing up and reaching for the overhead rack, somehow managed to dislodge Alvin's grip. It dropped fair and square on to the gaming dish and scattered the dice across the floor of the compartment. The language of the two old ladies surprised Alvin who rebuked Norbert for his clumsiness. By the time the dice had been retrieved the shuttle had whispered into the Paddington Terminal and the passengers were alighting.

The last Alvin saw of Margaret and Peggy they appeared to be heading towards the Terminal buffet accompanied, strangely enough, by the very man who had been so rude about Norbert. He pointed out this curious coincidence to the chimp who merely shrugged glumly and told Alvin he had been taken for a ride. 'That game was fixed,' he said. 'Some sort of magnetic trick, I suppose. I tried to warn you.'

Alvin was deeply shocked. 'You mean those two nice old ladies were cheating me? I don't believe it!'

'Suit yourself, son,' said Norbert, 'but if I hadn't dropped that grip when I did it's a safe bet you'd have been cleaned right out by now. How much did they milk you for?'

'Two hundred pounds,' said Alvin sadly. 'Are you saying that you dropped my bag on the table on *purpose*?'

Norbert chuckled. 'Pity I didn't think of doing it a bit sooner, wasn't it? Still, maybe it'll have taught you a lesson. Come on now, let's go and find out about that Croydon connection. And for Pete's sake, Alvin, keep your purse zipped into your inside pocket.'

They discovered that the electronic connection indicator was out of action, so Norbert sought out a fellow anthropoid on the Expressway staff and put the question to him. The uniformed chimp regarded Alvin curiously. 'Who's the pinkie?' he asked Norbert. 'Friend of yours?'

'He's a good lad,' said Norbert.

'Pleased to meet you, sir,' said Alvin and held out his hand.

The chimp rolled his eyes. 'Hey, d'you want t'get me the *sack*!' he hissed, and turning back to Norbert said: 'Just what kind of a goon *is* this?'

'He's a bit simple,' said Norbert, 'but one of the best. He doesn't mean any harm.'

'Glad to hear it,' said the other doubtfully. 'Well, what can I do for you, friend?'

Norbert explained again that they were anxious to get to Croydon and were wondering whether they should take a cab.

'You'll be lucky,' grunted the chimp. 'Don't you know there's a strike on?'

'No,' said Norbert.

'Well, there is. So I reckon your best bet would be to take the flow-way to Baker Street, hoof it up to Oxford Street, then round Hyde Park and try for a Suburban from the Kensington Terminus. Hang on a minute. Hey, Charlie, how's the South Suburban?'

'It was running this morning, Mose,' replied another ape approaching them. ''Bout two an hour, I think. What's the problem?'

'These two yokels want to get to Croydon.'

Charlie pushed back his cap and scratched his head. 'Flow-way to Baker Street then dahn t'the Dilly.'

'Not Kensington?'

'Dilly's safer, Mose. They're knockin' em off in daylight now rahnd the Park. Up to you, of course. Me, I'd have the Dilly.'

'Thanks,' said Norbert. 'Come on, Alvin.'

'Good luck,' grinned Mose. 'Rather you than me.'

They headed towards the main cloaca. 'Now you stick close to me, son,' instructed Norbert. 'If we get separated down here, you get off at Baker Street and wait for me there. Have you got that?'

Alvin nodded. 'Baker Street,' he repeated dutifully.

Norbert tugged his hat down over one eye, humped his shoulders and barged a way into the dense crowd which was struggling for standing room on the articulated roadway. Alvin clutched his grip and plunged after him. Within seconds they were being sucked down into one of the huge tiled tunnels, two fragments of a solid tide of human and anthropoid bodies which was being swept inexorably towards the heart of the city.

There was no problem about keeping their balance. The passengers were crammed so tightly together it would have been physically impossible to fall over. Electronic music, interspersed with raucous commercials, twanged and hummed through the fetid air. Somewhere ahead a woman began to shriek hysterically, but none of the passengers surrounding Alvin appeared in the least perturbed. Their eyes had the filmy, glazed look he had seen before only in the dead fish he sometimes found floating belly-upwards in Lake Tring.

Eventually a vast illuminated sign loomed up to inform them that they were approaching Baker Street. Norbert grabbed Alvin and began squirming his way towards the edge of the flow-way. He need not have bothered. A minute later the whole crowd surged off the track sweeping them up to the turnstiles whether they wanted to go there or not. Norbert thrust the plastic tags of their travel warrants into the scanner and then they were through.

Alvin drew what seemed to be his first breath for an hour. 'Is it always like that in the city, Norbert?' he enquired with a shudder.

'The Terminal links are the worst,' said Norbert, 'specially now there's a cab strike on. I daresay you'd get used to it in time.'

'But I've never *seen* so many people. Where do they all come from?'

'Well, there's over 50 million in Inner London for a start,' said Norbert restoring the travel warrants to his wallet and placing the wallet in an inside compartment of his brief case. 'And another 50 million come in from the suburbs every day.'

'But why don't they live in the country like we do?'

Norbert shrugged. 'Land's too precious, son, that's why. The other reason is they couldn't. Haven't you ever wondered why we never see more than a couple of hundred up at the lakes?'

'No,' said Alvin who hadn't.

'Well, people are conditioned to like what they've got. They have to be.'

'Conditioned to like *this*?' said Alvin, gazing around him at the seething multitude. 'How *can* they be?'

'Maybe not *this* particularly,' said Norbert, 'but to living in the Supercities. How else could you fit 350 millions into an island the size of ours?' He zipped up his case, locked it, and motioned with his head towards one of the street exits. 'Come on,' he grinned, 'let's go and find ourselves something to eat.'

7

THEY STEPPED OUT into the canyon that was Baker Street. Although it was still the middle of the afternoon the street lighting was already full on. Only on the very brightest of days could sufficient sunlight penetrate the stratospheric haze and filter down through the cab grid lattice which festooned the towering residential blocks to illuminate the roadway far below.

The first three eating houses they tried all displayed 'N.A.' (No Anthropoids) or 'H.O.' (Humans Only) notices in their windows, but the fourth proclaimed itself an open house and they went in.

It was one of a chain of middle-grade, self-service eateries called '*Horn of Plenty*'. They were to be found in all the Supercities under their motif of a buxom Ceres ladling an inexhaustible supply of appetizing goodies out of a giant shell. Within, above a battery of chromium lockers, mouth-watering, coloured stereoscopic images invited the hungry multitude to slot in their £10 pieces and help themselves to health. Alvin selected roast chicken with mushrooms and French fried. Norbert opted for 'Vegetarian's Delite'. Both turned out to be processed protein staple, artificially flavoured and coloured, and shaped to bear some crude resemblance to their remote ancestors.

The two travellers carried their purchases across to a vacant table and sat down. No sooner had they done so than faint, convivial sounds of eating and drinking seemed to enwrap them like mist: the tinkle of glassware and cutlery; anticipatory rustling of paper napkins; the crack of crisp breadsticks being broken; little 'oohs', 'ahs', and 'ums' of gustatory pleasure; and all interspersed with tiny, genteel, but unmistakable, sighs and burps of the well-fed.

Since all the food was in fact served in compartmented plastic trays and the only implements supplied were a solitary plastic spoon apiece, the management had elected to reinforce the *bon-viveur* illusion by triggering sonics to the seats and releasing minute amounts of selected pheromones through the ventilators.

Alvin was so intrigued that he stood up again only to discover that by so doing he had initiated a further automatic process whereby his half of the table-top began sliding into the wall carrying his tray with it. He sat down again just in time to retrieve it and to appreciate the force of the warning printed round the rim of his tray: '*Customers are respectfully requested not to vacate their seats during the course of their meal.*'

When Norbert had chomped his way stolidly through the last of his viridescent lettuce-type salad leaves he laid down his spoon, wiped his lips with his handkerchief and said: 'I think we might as well walk up to the Park. If we find the Suburbans aren't running, we'll still have plenty of time to get down to Piccadilly and try from there.'

'All right,' agreed Alvin. 'Whatever you say.'

Norbert inserted the tip of a prosthetic thumb into his mouth and delicately dislodged a morsel of synthetic beetroot from his palate. 'Doctor Pfizier told you why we're taking you to the M.O.P., did he?'

'Because of my libido,' said Alvin. 'Do you know what that is?'

'Mating urge,' grunted Norbert.

'Oh. Is that bad?'

'We-l-l,' said the chimp judiciously, 'I suppose it *might* be. If you let it.'

'Have you had it, Norbert?'

Norbert chuckled. 'All that's way behind me now, lad. I leave it to the youngsters. More important things to worry about. Mind you, I don't say there weren't times . . .' and he slipped into one of those thoughtful silences that were so familiar to Alvin.

'Doctor Somervell seemed to think I had immature sexual fantasies,' remarked Alvin, sucking the pseudo-flesh off a plastic wishbone and laying it back tidily on his tray. 'That was after I told her about the girl I saw yesterday. Before she made me take advantage of her.'

Norbert surfaced abruptly from his reverie. '*Who* did *what*, lad?'

Alvin blinked. 'Doctor Somervell did. I'm sure she meant it kindly though.'

'What happened?'

'I'm not really sure,' confessed Alvin. 'I couldn't see very well.'

'She turned the light out?'

'Oh no,' said Alvin. 'It all sort of happened under her clothes.'

'But you must have done *something*, lad?'

'No, I didn't, Norbert. She did it all. Honestly.'

'But you must – well, it doesn't really matter. How did Doctor Pfizier get to hear of it?'

'Oh he came in when she was sitting on top of me.'

Norbert who was not a powerful visualizer in the normal way found the demands of this particular scene almost overwhelming. 'Holy gorilla!' he murmured, which was the strongest epithet he ever allowed himself.

Alvin spooned in the last of his French frieds and washed them down with synthetic grape juice. 'Do you suppose Professor Poynter will want to do that too, Norbert?'

'I daresay she'll be prepared to take your word for it,' said the chimp. 'Now if you've finished we'd better be on our way.'

They descended once more into the street and found the sidewalk thronged with curious bystanders all gaping at some sort of parade which was passing down Baker Street towards Marble Arch. Since neither Alvin nor Norbert was particularly tall, all they could discern of the procession were the wobbling placards carried by the marchers. These seemed to embrace such a wide spectrum of concern from the ultra-violet of 'FREEDOM OF CHOICE!' to the infra-red of 'VOTES FOR APES!' that Norbert was moved to enquire of a spectator what the demonstration was about. 'Hampstead and Highgate Protestors' Rally,' he was told.

When five minutes had passed and still the procession showed no signs of coming to an end, Norbert had a sudden inspiration. Pulling Alvin with him by the arm, he squeezed his way through to the front of the crowd. Seizing the first opportune gap in the ranks he stepped boldly into the parade immediately behind a tall, thin, balding man of indeterminate age who was holding aloft a placard which read: 'CREWYS ROAD ANTI-VASECTOMY LEAGUE'. His companion, as tall and gangling as he was, though differentiated by a sparse beard, carried a similar sign inscribed: 'SAVE OUR SPERMS!' Norbert lifted his hat solemnly to them both and earned himself a friendly smile of welcome.

'First class turn out, isn't it?' observed the beardless standard bearer. 'You with the V.F.A. crowd?'

Norbert nodded and winked at Alvin.

'I believe they're up ahead somewhere,' said the beard. 'I daresay you might get through to them if you tried.'

Norbert shook his head to signify that he was quite happy where he was, whereupon the beardless one glanced back over his ranks and cried: 'Right! All together now! One, two, three! *Balls! Balls! We need balls ... Balls! Balls! We need balls ... Balls! Balls! We need balls! ...*'

Alvin and Norbert found themselves chanting with the rest, their heels drumming a heart-warming rhythm from the compo-surfaced roadway. Like errant snowflakes a few shreds of torn-up paper fluttered down from the canyon walls far above their heads, metamorphosing into brilliant multi-coloured butterflies as they slid and paused and twirled above the rainbow neon signs which advertised the Dream Arcades of Portman Square. '*Balls!*' howled Alvin, his innocent blue eyes glittering with the happy excitement of this new-found solidarity, and '*Balls!*' thundered Norbert doffing his hat left and right to all and sundry, '*Balls! Balls! We need balls!*'

They swung round the corner into Oxford Street and saw ahead of them the narrow crack that was the sky broadening out and deepening into something almost approaching blue over the fringes of Hyde Park. Four hundred yards ahead the banners of the procession leaders scooped up the exhausted sunbeams and batted them like shuttlecocks from one to another as they snaked around Marble Arch and into the Park. From the sidewalks the massed onlookers cheered derisively or just stared apathetically, while the white helmets of Security Guards bobbed like ping-pong balls as they cantered up and down the line on their electric prancers, their white stun probes couched like lances and their red and white gas pistols bouncing against their hips.

Norbert took advantage of a lull to put his lips to Alvin's ear and say: 'We'll drop out when we get to Marble Arch. It's only ten minutes from there to the station.'

'All right,' said Alvin concealing his disappointment as best he could. 'It's been fun, hasn't it?'

'We'll have a chorus or two of S.O.S.' called the man with the beard. 'Give it plenty of soul and take the time from me. Ready? One, two, three!' And with that he launched them dolefully into '*Save our Sperms*' to the ancient tune of *Three Blind Mice*.

> '*Save our sperms,*
> *Save our sperms,*
> *They may be germs,*
> *They may be germs,*
> *But why shouldn't they have a right to life?*
> *They're all a man's got to give to his wife!*
> *So save our forks from the government knife*
> *And save our sperms!*'

They sang it through three times and by the time they reached the final chorus they had also reached Marble Arch. At that very moment a scarlet flare trailing a cloud of dense pink smoke sailed up over the trees by Speakers' Corner. 'Oh dear, this looks like trouble,' muttered the tall beardless man as a posse of Security Guards galloped past on their prancers, stun probes at the ready.

35

Up ahead Alvin could see banners waving wildly under the trees. There was a lot of distant shouting and screaming.

'Come on, son,' said Norbert grimly, 'this is where we drop out.'

But it was already too late. Borne forward by the press of marchers behind them and hemmed into the roadway by the rapidly swelling crowds of spectators they found themselves swirled forward like so much unwilling flotsam into the vortex of a pitched battle. It was impossible for Alvin and Norbert to tell who was fighting whom, but judging by the way in which banners were being wielded as weapons on both sides, two opposing armies of protest seemed to have converged head on.

Not the least extraordinary aspect of the scene was the sudden appearance of the articulated So-Vi camera cranes. They stooped over the struggling mass like long-beaked water waders, pecking here and there as fancy dictated. Alvin gazed in astonishment as one of them soared high into the air, appeared to hover for a moment, then swooped down just as a solid placard bearing the one word 'LOVE' descended like a mediaeval battle-axe to cleave the bald pate of an elderly gentleman who, at the moment of impact, looked utterly astonished.

As for the Security Guards, instead of attempting to separate the antagonists, they had formed themselves into a sort of human arena, open only at either end to allow the opposing rearguards to join the fray. Once the last contingent was inside, the ring completed itself, and with levelled probes the Guards ensured that none of those inside got out.

Not that many of them seemed to want to, for those that did were treated to a whiff of agro-14 from a red gas pistol as soon as they approached the perimeter of the arena. This had the instantaneous effect of sending them rampaging back into the fray like the war horse who smelt the battle from afar and cried Ha! Ha! among the trumpets. It no longer mattered who was friend and who was foe; to bash, beat, club, strangle and claw was all that counted now.

In a quite remarkably short space of time there was no-one left standing. Men and women, young and old, were heaped dead, dying, maimed, or simply unconscious under the indifferent trees. In place of the wild berserker shouts of rage there were now only moans and whispers and the occasional bubbling gasp. The prosboces of the cameras probed fastidiously here and there seeking their last arty morsels – a child's gouged-out eye or a fingerless hand – before zooming out and up to diminish the perspective from high above.

A whistle was blown, the masked Guards brought their lances up, spun on their booted heels, and lowered their weapons among the hushed spectators. There was an immediate backward shuffle to get out of range. Another whistle blast and the Guards moved slowly forward, driving back the perimeter of the battle-field further and ever further until at last the crowd was dispersed.

8

IN THE THREE years which had elapsed since her traumatic experience with Alvin and his brothers, Professor Poynter had suffered from what can best be described as periodic formication of the conscience. She had gradually become convinced that she had acted in blind panic, engendered in her by a primitive sense of sexual outrage, at discovering herself to be standing, stark naked, in a technicians' washroom surrounded by half a dozen utterly astounded chimpanzees. To get there she had seemingly been instantaneously defabricated, reconstituted, and passed through a nine-inch wall of carbon-reinforced siliconized concrete, travelling in all a distance of some eight metres linear in a south-easterly direction. But instead of embracing the experience as a heaven-sent confirmation of her sixteen years' faith in the value of her experiment, her reaction had been to seize upon the first available cannister of azaguanine-12 and blindly blot out the perpetrators of the miracle. Admittedly the effects of her action had been infinitely more drastic than she had intended, but in her heart of hearts she knew, only too well, that even if that cannister had happened to contain triapsincyanide she would have used it just the same. This shameful realization was what she had been wearing next to her soul like a coconut-matting liberty bodice for 39 long months – the bitter knowledge that, at the moment of supreme crisis, her nerve had failed her, and she had behaved just like an ordinary woman.

Now at last a single glow-worm of hope seemed to have wriggled out of the ruins. Damnably, that nincompoop Pfizier had been hopelessly unspecific about the precise nature of Alvin's experience (there you go again, Miriam, blaming someone else when you know perfectly well that if *you* had dared to be more specific in the first place, Pfizier would have known what to look for!), but why on earth the stupid man should have harped so on the boy's awakening sexual proclivities when all *she* was concerned about was this single, possible (dare she even *say* the word?) *eidetic* manifestation, was almost beyond the bounds of comprehension. Still (credit where credit was due) the lad *should* have been 'null libido', and if he *wasn't* (and whatever else Pfizier wasn't, he had certainly been positive enough on *that* score!) then conceivably the A-12 erasure might not have been as complete as it had appeared on the encephalographic record. In which case . . .

The jingling carousel – which was what Professor Poynter's mind seemed to have become in the last eight hours – churned round and round in its restless circuit. Twice already she had videophoned Aldbury hoping to discover precisely when she could expect the clone to arrive, only to be told that, as far as they knew, he was safely on his way in the care of a trusted anthropoid named Norbert. She had hung about at the M.O.P. until 20.00 hours going over Alvin's electro-encephalogram again and again until she felt as if each individual squiggle on the chart had been scratched directly on to the surface of her own cortex. Finally, after leaving the strictest possible instructions that she was to be videophoned the instant the clone arrived, she had summoned a ministerial buggy and been driven to her home in Richmond where Hortense, her beautiful, 30-year-old Eurasian wife, was awaiting her.

The Professor found her curled up on the hydro-couch watching So-Vi. She was sipping at a tall tulip glass of vintage eroticon and smelt, deliciously, of almonds. 'You look bushed, my sweet,' she murmured. 'Come and sit down here and I'll fix you one of these.' She uncoiled her long legs, stood up, and willowed her way across the room to the cocktail cabinet.

Professor Poynter subsided thankfully into the couch and let out her breath in a weary sigh. 'You'll never guess what's turned up, petal.'

'Then tell me,' said Hortense sensibly.

'One of my four clones might – just *might*, mind you – have begun to regenerate!'

'But that's marvellous!'

'Isn't it? I can hardly dare to believe it. I'm not breathing a word to a soul yet, of course.'

'When will you know for sure?' asked Hortense, replacing the stopper in the crystal decanter and lifting the filled goblet delicately by its slender stem.

'Tonight, I hope.'

'Tonight! Explique moi, chérie!'

'They're phoning me from the lab the minute he arrives. I'll go over and collect him.'

' "Collect him"? You mean you're going to bring him back *here*?'

'Yes, of course. It's the obvious thing to do. I can run the tests just as well here – far better, in fact. Furthermore I suspect a sympathetic environment may prove absolutely critical. You don't mind, do you?'

'Why should I mind, my love? Here's your drink.'

'Bless you,' murmured the Professor, accepting the proffered glass and smiling up into the dark eyes above her. 'And what have you been doing with yourself?'

Hortense shrugged. 'Nothing very exciting. Watching that. "*Your Day*", isn't it? Shall I switch it off?'

Professor Poynter's eyes actively registered the video-screen for the first time. Viewed from high above, two spiky millipedes of protestors were advancing steadily upon each other – the 'Hampstead and Highgaters' along Oxford Street and the 'Bermondsey and Batterseas' along Park Lane.

Hortense moved across to the set and was about to switch it off when Professor Poynter said: 'No, leave it a moment, pet. Douglas Crowe was telling me about this the other day. It's something *Minisoc* have dreamt up – I think he called it a field trial for manipulated aggression.'

'And what's that when it's been processed?' asked Hortense.

'Crowe and his friends have been culturing anti-socials in each district for the past year. Now they're ready to see if the dissidents can't be induced to eliminate each other by artificial over-stimulation of the adrenal system. It's an interesting theory.'

Hortense pulled a face and moved back to join her husband on the couch. 'It looks as if it's working, doesn't it?' she observed. 'Ugh! How beastly!'

'Fascinating,' breathed the Professor. 'It really does look as if they might have a winner this time. My goodness! Did you see that?'

'Oh, *really*!' protested Hortense. 'Must we?'

'But this is tremendously significant, my pet. Manipulated aggression on a really worth-while socially therapeutic scale.'

'It's *horrible*,' muttered Hortense making a feeble attempt to look the other way and finding that her eyes were drawn back to the carnage in spite of herself. 'They've all gone mad! Ooh, *look* at that!'

As the cameras zoomed in to proffer their succulent tit-bits of stereoscopic anguish to millions of enthralled viewers throughout the Western network, Hortense finally succeeded in closing her eyes.

They were still shut tight when she heard a gasp of astonishment and felt her husband's fingers tighten suddenly round her wrist. 'No, it *can't* be!' exclaimed Professor Poynter.

Hortense opened her eyes and quickly shut them again. 'Oh, *do* switch it off!' she wailed. 'It's making me feel ill.'

Rather to her surprise the Professor got up from the couch and did as she was asked, but then, instead of resuming her seat and indulging Hortense with the consolatory caresses she was expecting, she disappeared into the study to emerge, a minute later, bearing the album that Sir Gordon Loveridge had presented to her back in '69.

'What on earth have you got there?' demanded Hortense.

'Just look at this,' said the Professor stabbing her forefinger at the bland features of one of the four clones (it was Bruce, actually, but there was no way of telling them apart except by their clothes) 'and now take a look at this.' She stepped across to the So-Vi, pushed the playback button, held it for a second or two, then thumbed the viewer. After flicking back and forth for a few moments she grunted triumphantly: 'There! That's the one!'

The picture that had materialized within the screen was a 3-dimensional close-up of a moon-faced youth, with remarkably protuberant ears, in the process of being slowly throttled by an obviously enraged ape. Allowing for the differences of facial expression, i.e. slight surprise in the album and utter astonishment on the screen, the similarity between the two sets of features was certainly extraordinary.

'*Could* it be him?' asked Hortense curiously.

'Well, if it isn't him, it's certainly *one* of them,' said the Professor. 'What's more it would explain why he hasn't turned up.'

'But what was he doing there?'

'There are some things, my pet, which even I can hardly be expected to answer – yet,' said the Professor, clicking off the picture and striding purposefully towards the door of the apartment.

'Where are you off to now?' wailed Hortense.

'To try to locate him, of course.'

'But he'll be *dead*!'

'We don't *know* that, do we? And even if he is, he'll still be *some* use to me.'

'Oh really, Miriam, this is *absurd*! At least have some dinner first.'

But Professor Poynter was already on her way.

9

ALVIN WAS NOT dead as it happened, only very, very unconscious. His recovery of his senses was a weirdly unreal process in which, like some huge, indolent fish he seemed to rise slowly to the surface, gulp, and then sink as slowly back again into the cloudy depths. This was repeated at least a dozen times with the intervals between the gulps growing shorter and shorter until, finally, with one heart-rending groan he opened his reluctant eyes.

His first coherent thought was that, wherever else he might be, he was certainly not lying in his bunk at Aldbury. Directly above him, through a sort of macabre gothic arch formed – though Alvin did not realize it – from the crotch of a stiffening Highgate Quaker, he glimpsed a salmon-pink wisp of cirrostratus tangled like a feather in the topmost twigs of a dead elm. As he peered up at it disbelievingly it faded slowly from his sight and its place was taken by a small bird which, after emitting a couple of wistful *cheep-cheeps*, fluffed out its feathers and prepared to settle down for the night. 'Hey!' croaked Alvin in sudden alarm. 'Hey! Help!'

From the shambles around him his appeal evoked a few feeble groans. These continued for a few moments then died dispiritedly away.

Alvin somehow succeeded in dislodging the Quaker's right thigh from its resting place on his own right shoulder and struggled up into a sitting position. His throat was extremely painful and he found considerable difficulty in swallowing. For hundreds of yards in all directions about him the gentle evening shadows were congealing around untidy heaps of bodies from which the splintered shafts of placard handles projected haphazardly like ill-directed *banderillas*. As he surveyed the dismal scene, uselessly but quite understandably, Alvin began to weep. Through the shifting lens of his tears the scattered corpses gained, for a little while, an illusory animation.

Staggering to his feet he began to pull despairingly at odd arms and legs, as though by doing so he might galvanize them back into more than just a semblance of life. So it was that, by sheer chance, he stumbled upon a leg that seemed to respond to his tugging.

Apologizing to the dead for his intrusion, he began frenziedly dragging aside the corpses that were covering the body to which the limb was attached and succeeded at last in lugging it clear. How can one hope to convey his delirious delight when he discovered that the object of his efforts was none other than Norbert? Flinging himself upon his friend he began at once to administer the kiss-of-life, a technique in which – despite Doctor Somervell's contention – he had long ago acquired a considerable degree of expertise.

After five minutes of dizzying effort the chest of the chimp began a fluttering rise and fall, whereupon Alvin, seizing him by the shoulders of his jacket, dragged him backwards across the trampled grass, propped him up against the bole of a tree and ran as fast as he could to seek further assistance.

He had covered no more than a couple of hundred yards when he found his headlong flight was blocked by a high black wall. This was a pre-fabricated palisade which the authorities had erected round the battlefield while Alvin was still lying insensible. It was now stretched to left and right in an unbroken line enclosing a roughly oval area about a third of a mile long and a quarter of a mile wide.

Trotting disconsolately round this black perimeter trying to find some way out, Alvin came upon a fountain at which he was able to relieve his aching throat. A short distance beyond the fountain was a public videophone booth. This, like the fountain, had got itself included within the scope of the fence.

With a display of initiative which would certainly have surprised his friends at Aldbury Alvin thrust his way into the booth and confronted the instrument. While he was wondering who to summon to his aid his attention was caught by a glocard riveted to the wall: 'DESPERATE? LIFE PROVING TOO MUCH FOR YOU? CALL SAMARITANS 0000.'

Convinced that his prayers had been answered Alvin delved into his pocket, discovered a £2 piece, thrust it into the metal slot and pressed the 'o' button four times.

Thirty seconds later the screen had cleared. He waited impatiently for a face to surface from its depths, but all that happened was that a feminine voice breathed gently from the speaker into his ear: 'You need our help?'

'Oh, *yes*,' cried Alvin fervently. '*Please.*'

'You've lost your nerve, have you?'

'Eh?'

'You found you couldn't go through with it?'

'What?'

'You *do* want our help?'

'Yes, yes,' cried Alvin.

'All right. Now where exactly are you?'

'I'm not sure. Marble Arch, I think.'

'How high?'

'?'

'How high up are you?' repeated the voice patiently.

Alvin looked down at his feet in some bewilderment. 'I don't know,' he said. 'About half a metre, I suppose.'

In his ear he heard something that sounded improbably like a chuckle. 'Oh dear,' said the voice, 'then it's not much use jumping, is it?'

'Jumping?'

'It *is* the simplest usually. I can talk you right out then. I'm very good at that. But don't worry. We'll think of something.'

'You'll come and help?'

'I *can*,' said the voice doubtfully. 'But it *is* rather awkward just now. I'm on emergency, you see.'

'But this *is* an emergency!' cried Alvin. 'We need help right away.'

' "We"? Aren't you alone, then?'

'Oh no. There's heaps of us.'

'And you *all* want help?'

'Well, not *all*. A lot of them are dead.'

'I *see*. You had a pact?'

'Attacked? I don't know *how* it happened. *Do* come.'

There was a pause, then: 'How many of you are there?'

'I'm not sure. There must be hundreds.'

'*Hundreds!* Are you serious?'

'They're everywhere,' said Alvin desperately. 'All over the place. It's like – like . . . ' but he didn't know what it was like and could only shrug helplessly.

'All right,' said the voice, 'I'll come. Where are you calling from? If it's a booth there'll be a number.'

'Yes,' said Alvin. 'Hyde Park X013.'

'Hang on a moment . . . Yes, I've got it. Why, it's just down below me. I'll need a couple of minutes to get my calls transferred and then I'll be with you. *How* many did you say?'

'Hundreds,' said Alvin.

'Yes, that's what I thought you said. Well, I'll bring what I can. See you.'

44

'Goodbye,' said Alvin.

He replaced the earphone on its rest and stepped outside. He saw that the sun had died leaving a blood red smear low down in the western sky, and that a single star had managed to drill its way through the overcast. He went back to the fountain, drank some more water, then took off one of his boots, filled it from the marble basin and carried it across the littered grass to Norbert.

Alvin splashed some of the water over the wheezing ape, then prised open his mouth and poured the rest inside. Norbert groaned and coughed and opened one bloodshot eye.

'Are you all right, Norbert?'

The eye closed again.

'Norbert? Norbert, wake up! *Please!*'

The other eye opened reluctantly and acknowledged the clone. 'Wasser marrer?'

'I thought you were dead,' said Alvin.

The first eye opened again. 'I,' groaned Norbert, then paused as if to regain his balance, 'I am the Resurrection and the Life.'

'No, you're not, Norbert.'

'Was it not you who baptized me in the Waters of Righteousness?' muttered the chimp.

'Shall I go and get some more?' said Alvin, squinting into his damp boot.

Norbert pressed his plastic thumbs tenderly against his temples. 'Aieee,' he sighed dejectedly. 'My head's splitting!'

The words were hardly uttered when Alvin heard a high-pitched whistling noise in the air above them. Looking up he saw a slender female shape briefly silhouetted against the glow of the west. He jumped up, dragged on his soaking boot and galloped back in the direction of the fountain. 'Hi, there!' he shouted. 'Hi! Hi!'

The airborne figure described a graceful aerial arabesque and came to earth on the grass a few yards away from him, the jets on her A-G harness expiring with a regretful hiss. As Alvin pounded up she palmed back her short brown hair, twitched her tunic straight, then smiled and held out her hand. 'My name's Cheryl,' she said. 'I'm your Samaritan.'

In the very act of reaching out to take the proffered hand Alvin seemed to become transfixed. His mouth drooped open and an expression of beatific imbecility spread itself slowly across his face like melted butter across a muffin. 'But ... but ... but it's *you*!' he gulped.

Cheryl's exquisite head tilted like a quizzical blossom on her slender neck; whereupon the last faint tendrils of the twilight touched her eyes and transformed them into gleaming pools of green chalcedony. Something in the boy's tone, some note of wonder or worship whose like she had never encountered before, made her frown and step backwards a pace. 'What do you mean?' she said. 'Of course it's me.'

'*Spirodella polyrhiza*,' whispered the moonstruck clone. 'Eyes like *spirodella polyrhiza* and hair the colour of bog peat.' So saying he subsided to his knees before her, garnered up her hand in both of his and pressed it reverently to his lips.

'Holy hemlock!' whistled Cheryl. 'You weren't joking about needing my help, were you?'

IO

At the very instant when Alvin was pressing his adoring lips to Cheryl's slender fingers, Professor Poynter finally succeeded in making video contact with Doctor Douglas Crowe of the Ministry of Sociology. She found him in a state of effervescent elation. 'Miriam!' he cried. 'How nice to see you! Wasn't it *sensational*?'

'Most impressive, Douglas. The Minister must be very pleas –'

'Absolutely *delighted*! I've just had him on. We're all going down to the Park to take a body-count at 21.30. I say, if you're interested, why don't you come along too?'

'That's just what I was hoping you might suggest.'

'Excellent!'

'Douglas, I don't suppose you happen to know if there were any survivors?'

'Bound to be one or two, I suppose – juveniles mostly, no doubt. But I must say that the results so far have quite exceeded all our expectations. Agro-14 really *is* sensational! There's no other word for it! At least fifty per cent of them simply uttered a couple of whoops of rage and dropped dead in their tracks. Talk about the enemy within! Incidentally, Rodney seems convinced we'll soon be able to cut the conditioning period to six months – maybe even *three*! I tell you, augmented adrenal hypertension is *in*, Miriam – *right* in!'

'Douglas, I do hope you won't mind my asking this, but are you absolutely positive that all the participants *had* been conditioned?'

'Good Lord, yes! We had the registers double checked before march off. Anyway, the routes were cordoned off the whole time.'

'But I suppose it is *just* possible that someone could have slipped through and joined in?'

'Well, if they did it only goes to prove that agro-14's even better than we thought, doesn't it? But I don't really think it's on, Miriam. The urban district group loyalty's far too strong. Take it from me, the only ones there were there because they *wanted* to be there. But what makes you ask?'

Professor Poynter temporized. 'It was just that I thought I might have glimpsed someone I knew. Obviously I was mistaken.'

Doctor Crowe grinned sardonically. 'Now don't tell me you've taken to consorting with social dissidents, Professor. It doesn't really sound like your scene at all.'

'No, of course not. That's what made me ask about your security arrangements.'

'Believe me, Miriam, no one joins a protest march unless they want to protest.'

'No, I suppose not.'

'There's no "suppose" about it. A behavioural pattern's a behavioural pattern. You know that.'

Professor Poynter nodded. 'What time did you say you were going along, Douglas?'

'We'll be opening up the can at 21.30. I aim to start the autopsies around midnight. Why don't you come along here first and let me introduce you to the Minister?'

'That's very kind of you.'

'Not at all. There's bound to be several people you know. Lovelick's coming, and Jerry Forth and – Hello, that looks like a call in on my red band. We'll see you in half an hour then, Miriam. Bye-bye for now.'

''Bye,' responded Professor Poynter automatically and the screen blanked out.

Unknown to either of the two scientists, three miles away in the subterranean Censorship Vaults of the Ministry of Social Security – universally known as MOSS – the videophone random censor had selected for security analysis the very conversation which we have just recorded.

Along with a hundred others the casual exchanges were even now in the process of being filter screened for audible and visual evidence of possible social subversion. Telltale needles waggled across calibrated dials as each syllable of each phrase was weighed and sifted, not simply for its overt verbal content but for its give-away emotional undertones. An eye-blink, a cough, a syllabic stress, a significant pause – these could add up to an indictment just as damning as any signed and witnessed confession.

Long before the final farewell was spoken a crimson warning light had started to throb like an inflamed carbuncle above the cabinet which was monitoring Professor Poynter's call. At the same time no fewer than 57 of the other 99 cabinets were also having luminous hysterics about the seditious diets they were being asked to digest. This overwhelming proof of universal guilt was brought within manageable limits by a random selector which came into action once every five minutes and chose from among those already chosen. A single light changed from red to purple and the other 57 all switched themselves off, thereby automatically erasing the evidence of subconscious subversion which had been so ingeniously harnessed to trigger their illumination.

Up to this point no human intelligence had been involved and even Copperfield, the anthropoid Master Sergeant who super-intended the Censorship Vaults, was scarcely alive to the progress of events. After all, each hour of the day and night produced on average its quota of forty potential subversives, a total of some nine hundred and sixty in every twenty-four hours, or just over three hundred and fifty thousand each year in London alone.

It was to winnow this monstrous crop of human frailty that Copperfield, acting entirely on his own initiative, had devised a further refinement in the process of selection. It had the simplicity which is the hall-mark of genius and consisted of choosing a secret code word for each hour of the day and programming a computer to check the recorded conversations against this particular word. Those that did not employ it in that particular hour were summarily erased. If more than five conversations employed it then those that used it least were erased. By this simple and ingenious method Master Sergeant Copperfield ensured that the full powers of the MOSS security forces could be deployed with maximum effect against a minimum of suspects.

On Wednesday, September 4th, for the sixty minutes between 20.00 hours and 21.00 hours the word Copperfield's computer was seeking for happened to be '*minister*'.

As a result of its analysis, at 23.00 hours a green alert went out for a security check to be kept on the movements of a newly ordained Baptist chaplain ape by the name of Wilberforce who lived in Cheam, together with his friend Labricorne, a sub-deacon in the Southwark diocese; two pious Unitarian sisters called Mirabelle and Connie Trugger who had made a point of video-phoning each other at the same time every Wednesday evening for the past 37 years; Doctor Douglas Crowe the young white hope of *Minisoc*; and Professor Miriam Poynter, O.B.E., D.Sc., etc. etc., Senior Geneticist at the Ministry of Procreation.

Such were the destinies that shaped one's end in A.D. 2072. *Dominus vobiscum!*

II

ALTHOUGH ALL SAMARITANS carried in their knapsacks sufficient hemlock, hellebore, henbane, aconite, curare, cyanide, hyoscine, strychnine and their numerous derivatives to soothe the troubled breasts of the most demanding of their clients, they were, by virtue of their Oath of Office and – let us admit it – a certain archaic squeamishness on the part of the Mother of Parliaments, expressly forbidden to administer these noxious substances themselves. They could lead the horse to the Lethean water – were, indeed, paid handsomely to do so – but they were not sanctioned to pour the stuff down his throat. Consequently, as Cheryl gazed down pensively into the mutely pleading eyes of the supplicant before her, she was simply debating inwardly which of her potent armoury of drowsy syrups would best medicine him to that sweet sleep from which there is no awakening.

While she pondered she fondled his ears abstractedly, much as in an earlier age her forebears might have stroked an adoring puppy who is about to be put down, and, as she did so she was vaguely touched to see that his eyes had filled with happy tears. Her fingers relinquished his ear and strayed in a cobweb of a caress across his forehead and down his damp cheek. 'Now more than ever seems it rich to die,' she murmured, 'To cease upon the midnight with no pain . . .' while a little voice inside her head computed busily: 'Weight approx. 125 lb unclothed. Age 18 plus, so circulation presumably good. Say Hemlock f.f. 1/10th gr. admin. oral.'

She patted Alvin on the head, slipped her knapsack from her shoulders, unzipped it and began rummaging inside. From somewhere at the bottom she produced a pale blue phial which she unstoppered by a deft finger-twist and from it shook two small capsules into her palm. These she proffered to Alvin. He peered down at them with some perplexity and then back to her again. 'Go on,' she urged gently. 'Take them.'

'What are they?'

'They're to make you sleep.'

'But I don't want to sleep.'

'Yes, you do.'

'No, I don't.'

'You know you do.'

'No, really.'

'Yes.'

'No.'

'Oh damn!' exclaimed Cheryl gnawing her bewitching lip with ill-concealed vexation. 'What have I done wrong this time?'

'I'm sorry,' said Alvin, 'but perhaps you've got something for a sore throat?'

'These,' said Cheryl, rolling the capsules in her palm, 'will cure sore throats wonderfully, to say nothing of headaches, toothaches, heartaches and all the thousand natural shocks that flesh is heir to.'

'But they'll make me go to sleep. That's what you said. I don't want to go to sleep.'

Cheryl drew a deep breath. 'Now look here – what *is* your name?'

'Alvin,' said Alvin.

'Now look here, Alvin. I want to help you, really I do. But I can't help you unless you're prepared to co-operate. Right? Now you want to die and you've asked me to –'

'Die! Who said I wanted to die?'

'Why, you did!'

'I *didn't*! I don't want to die.'

'You *don't*? Oh *no*! That really is *too* bad!' And in her frustration Cheryl stamped her dainty foot quite hard on the bruised grass.

Alvin had a sudden stroke of pure inspiration. 'Not now I've seen *you*, I don't.'

'That's *ridiculous*!'

'But it's true,' he insisted. 'Ever since I saw you yesterday I've ... well, everything's been somehow ... I don't know ...'

'Do you mean to tell me that – that all this begging for help was just a *hoax*?'

'Oh *no*!' cried Alvin, suddenly remembering why he had summoned her. 'Look over there!'

Cheryl screwed up her eyes and peered into the gloom. 'Great Morpheus!' she whispered. 'Are those *bodies*?'

'Yes,' said Alvin.

Cheryl took a pace towards them and then appeared to hesitate. 'But how did it *happen*?'

'I don't know,' said Alvin. 'When I woke up they were like that. Norbert's the only one who's still alive. He's over by that tree.'

Like a kitten stalking a sparrow Cheryl stole forward. Alvin picked up the knapsack and hurried after her. 'We were in a sort of parade,' he panted, 'with banners and everything. Everyone was singing and shouting. Then we got here and they all seemed to go mad. At least I *think* that's what happened.'

Cheryl reached the first pile of corpses and stopped to examine it with a professional eye. When she straightened up Alvin touched her gently on the arm. 'Norbert's over there,' he said.

She allowed him to lead her into the gloomy sanctuary of the trees. The sheer magnitude of the massacre seemed temporarily to have stunned her. 'But I don't understand it,' she said. 'I just don't under*stand* it.'

'This is Cheryl, Norbert,' said Alvin. 'She's the one I saw yesterday. She's going to help us.'

Norbert heaved himself up on to his knees. 'An angel of light!' he exclaimed rapturously. 'She has been sent to lead us out of the Valley of the Shadow.'

'Oh dear,' said Cheryl, 'I'm afraid there's been some mistake.'

'You mean you *won't* help us?' said Alvin incredulously.

'But you don't understand! I'm a Samaritan. All I'm supposed to do is to help people who want to die.'

The anthropoid and the clone regarded her in wide-eyed disbelief. 'You are undoubtedly an angel,' said Norbert. 'I admit I have never seen one before but I recognized you immediately. You are now testing us before you succour us in the hour of our need. My lifelong faith in your existence has at last been rewarded.'

Cheryl hardly knew whether to laugh or cry. The only sensible course would be to jet off and leave them, but somehow she just couldn't bring herself to do it. It was as though she could feel all the incommensurable weight of that host of silent cadavers pressing down upon her. In the midst of such a superabundance of death, she, Death's official handmaiden, found herself faltering. 'But what do you expect me to *do*?' she wailed.

'Help us to get out of here,' said Alvin. 'Please.'

'But what's stopping you?'

'The fence is,' said Alvin. 'It's too high to climb over.'

'Isn't there a gate?'

'I've been all the way round. There's no way out at all.'

'Then how did you get in?'

'It wasn't there when we came in.'

'Fear not,' said Norbert. 'She will get us out. Put your trust in the Lord.'

Cheryl realized that she was still clutching the two capsules she had prescribed for Alvin. She brushed them off her palm on to the grass. 'All right,' she said, 'I'll lift you over. But that's all. We're not supposed to do it, but it's almost dark now. I don't suppose anyone will see us.'

She thrust the phial of hemlock back into her knapsack, shrugged it on to her back, then led the way purposefully towards the fountain. 'Where do you come from?' she asked.

'Aldbury,' said Alvin.

'Where's that?'

Norbert told her it was to the north-west of London.

'And what are you doing down here?'

In the darkness Norbert's honest brow puckered into a gloomy frown. He realized they must have left Aldbury to go *somewhere*. But where? A lungful of agro-14 had transformed what had once been bright with purpose into a cloudy negation. What's more his head ached abominably.

'Well?' prompted Cheryl. 'Are you on holiday?'

Alvin, who had been waiting for Norbert to supply the required information, seized his opportunity. 'Yes,' he said, 'that's right. We are, aren't we, Norbert?'

'Uh?' grunted Norbert dubiously.

'Where are you staying?'

Alvin's mind seemed to leap into overdrive. 'Near here,' he said. 'Near you.'

'The Cumberland?'

'Yes. Yes, that's right.'

'But the Cumberland's H.O.'

'Oh, is it? Well, where do *you* live?'

'Me? Bristol Street.'

'Is that H.O. too?'

'It's not a hotel.'

'Well, there then,' said Alvin brightly. 'That's where we're staying too, isn't it, Norbert?'

'Uh?' muttered Norbert.

'Oh yes?' said Cheryl suspiciously. 'Since when?'

Alvin scratched his head furiously. Having been vouchsafed his vision the only thing that mattered now was to keep hold of her. Why, oh why hadn't Doctor Pfizier taught him how to lie convincingly? 'Oh please let us stay with you!' he cried.

'*With me!* You must be crazy!'

'I can cook,' pleaded Alvin wildly, 'and wash up, and clean and chop wood and . . . and take advantage of you if you'd like me to. Oh please, please let me, beautiful Cheryl.'

Cheryl's laugh rose like a stream of silvery bubbles through the night air. 'Let you *what*?'

'Cook and clean and chop –'

'No. The other thing.'

'Take advantage,' whispered Alvin and his ears glowed shyly in the darkness like a pair of luminous raspberry lollies.

'That's what I thought you said,' giggled Cheryl.

'Then you'll let me?'

'Indeed I won't. I'll do just what I said I would and that's all. Come on. Who's first?'

'You go, Norbert,' choked Alvin, turning away to hide his gushing tears.

'Put your arms round my neck,' Cheryl instructed the chimp, 'and hang on tight. If you let go it's your own funeral.'

Norbert did as he was commanded. There was a moment's pause then Alvin heard a shrill hissing like a whistling kettle coming to the boil. Out of the corner of his watering eye he saw them rise, become a brief, denser darkness against the sky, and vanish over the top of the palisade. At that moment his sense of loss was considerably more poignant than any he had ever known.

True to her word, a minute later Cheryl was back. 'Quick!' she said. 'There's something going on over there.'

As she spoke they both heard the distant droning of heavy duty electric motors. The inspection convoy from the Ministry of Sociology was trundling along Park Lane. Alvin flung his arms about Cheryl's neck and for the first time in his life experienced the delight of clasping a girl to his breast. Unfortunately his ecstasy was short-lived, for with a shriek like a de-racinated mandrake the A-G jets whisked them into the air.

They cleared the top of the palisade by a good twenty metres and had just begun their descent when a searchlight sliced across the park and pinned them like some grotesque silver beetle against the buttressed outer wall of the stockade. From somewhere in the outer darkness a loud hailer barked a command to halt. 'Let go, you goop!' hissed Cheryl. 'I'm not having any part of this.'

But either from fear of breaking his neck or anguish at the thought of losing her, Alvin clung on the tighter. The next thing he knew they were both five hundred feet up in the air and the wind was pummelling at his ears like a pair of demented fists. Far below them the searchlight swept disconsolately back and forth among the tree tops. Alvin took one look down then squeezed his eyes shut and, for extra security, locked his legs tightly around hers. Astonishingly, Cheryl began to laugh. 'Why didn't you let go, you idiot? Now look at the mess we're in.'

But Alvin wasn't looking at anything. His nose was buried in the soft, perfumed flesh just below her left ear. As far as he was concerned, he was nine tenths of the way to Paradise. 'Are you really an angel?' he enquired.

'Oh, shut up.'

Experimentally, Alvin poked out the tip of his tongue and, very, very delicately licked the lobe of her ear. He thought it tasted rather like peanut butter.

12

CROUCHED IN THE clump of laurels where Cheryl had deposited him, Norbert heard the iron voice of authority and peeped out fearfully through the leaves just in time to see Alvin shooting up like a champagne cork towards the London ceiling. He muttered a prayer for their safe landing and wondered what would happen next.

The searchlight flicked across the palisade, probed among the trees, and then seemed to shrink as the truck on which it was mounted rolled forward and came to a halt some twenty yards from the fence. Two other vehicles purred up alongside, reached out with their articulated claws and lifted away a complete section of the prefabricated enclosure which they proceeded to stack on the back of the searchlight wagon. As soon as the wall was breached the three vehicles moved to one side and continued dismantling while a convoy of some twenty assorted trucks drove through the gap into the enclosure. Within minutes, portable floodlights were bathing the arena in a cold, greenish-white glow, while in place of the rapidly vanishing wall, a ring of helmeted Security Guards sprouted up like crash-cultured snowdrops.

Professor Poynter stepped down on to the matted grass and gazed about her incredulously. The technical miracle of 3-D So-Vi had in no way prepared her for this appalling reality. She was reminded nauseatingly of a Gustave Doré engraving of the aftermath of Waterloo which had given her nightmares in her childhood. The faint hope she had been nourishing that her clone might somehow have survived the holocaust wilted and died as her stupefied eye wandered along the untidy heaps of slain. 'Astonishing, isn't it, Professor?' enquired an amiable voice at her ear and she turned to find the Minister himself beaming at her.

She nodded and tried to look alert and intelligent.

'As a piece of field research I must say I find it *most* impressive,' he burbled. 'I only wish the P.M. could have been here to see it. Just between the two of us I've wondered once or twice recently whether young Crowe wasn't laying it on a bit thick with his agro-14. I mean to say, to a non-technical chap like me a Sika deer's one thing and a human being's another, but now, damn it, he's converted me absolutely. By employing adrenal-hypertension to weed out the social misfits there's no reason at all why we shouldn't be able to double our density over the next fifty years.' He giggled. 'You might almost say the sky's the limit now, eh?'

Professor Poynter managed a sickly smile and then blenched as a floater loaded with untidily severed limbs was guided past to a waiting freezer truck.

The Minister, observing her expression, clucked compassionately. 'I usually find it helps to think of it simply as highgrade animal protein,' he said. 'Ah, here comes Douglas now.'

Doctor Crowe's white lab coat already looked as if it had seen hard service in an abattoir, but his eyes were sparkling with boyish enthusiasm as he strode up to them. 'Well, Sir Harold, did I exaggerate?'

'No, dear boy, you most certainly did not. I've just been saying to Professor Poynter here that you've completely converted me to agro-14. You and Rodney have every right to congratulate yourselves. This really does look like the break-through we've all been waiting for.'

'It's good of you to say so, sir. At least it's proved the principle's sound and that's the main thing. A couple more full-scale trials like this and we'll really be in business.'

'Have you found any survivors yet?' asked Professor Poynter faintly.

'Four so far,' said Crowe. 'All juveniles. That makes sense of course. Even with conditioning as intensive as ours has been, adrenal development can't be pushed effectively below a certain limit. But it's beginning to look as though we'll end up with well over 95 per cent mortality. That's considerably above our most optimistic estimate.'

'Might I have a look at the ones who survived?'

'Help yourself. They're being oxygenated in the resuscitation unit. It's over there.' Doctor Crowe waved his hand towards the trees under which, a few brief minutes before, Norbert had lain.

Professor Poynter nodded her thanks and moved away. As she did so she was surprised by an unfamiliar prickling sensation located along her eyelids. Exploring with her fingertips she was bewildered to find that she was crying. 'How odd,' she thought. 'Can the lachyrymal glands really respond independently of physical or emotional stimulus? I must remember to ask Gordon.'

But it was not only her tear glands which were behaving oddly. Instead of stopping at the resuscitation unit her legs insisted on carrying her straight past it and on across the grass towards the patrolling perimeter Guards. Since their orders related only to keeping people out they stood aside to let her past and she marched on blindly into the darkness beyond.

Norbert who was still lurking in the shrubbery, saw an elderly woman advancing straight towards him and concluded, naturally enough, that he had been spotted. Just to be quite sure he waited till she was no more than five yards away, then raised his arms above his head and stood up.

Had she not been suffering from acute hysteric shock, Professor Poynter, confronted by such an apparition, might have reacted very differently. As it was Norbert's materialization seemed perfectly in keeping with the sort of insanity she had just witnessed. She came to an unsteady halt and blinked the tears from her eyes. 'Who are you?' she enquired wearily.

'I'm Norbert, ma'am,' replied the ape politely.

'And what are you doing in that bush, Norbert?'

'Hiding, ma'am.'

'Is it a good place to hide in?'

'Ma'am?'

'I asked if it was a good place to hide in.'

This was what Norbert had thought she had said but it had seemed somewhat too improbable. 'I hardly know how to answer, ma'am,' he said hesitantly. 'But since you have discovered me, I should say that it wasn't.'

Professor Poynter nodded approvingly at the logic of his answer. 'Then there is really no point in my joining you, is there?'

'No, ma'am,' agreed Norbert, taking a chance and lowering his arms. 'Were you looking for somewhere to hide?'

'To hide?' repeated Professor Poynter vaguely. 'I don't really know . . . you see I'm not feeling very . . . well . . . I . . .'

Norbert sprang out of his sanctuary just in time to catch her as her knees buckled beneath her. He was painfully aware that some two hundred yards away were a great many people who would consider only one possible interpretation for such a situation. But although common prudence counselled him to put as much distance as possible as quickly as possible between himself and this unfortunate woman, he had never been an ape who placed the preservation of his own skin before what he considered to be his Christian duty. He stooped, hoisted her over his shoulder and set off at a steady lope in the direction of the Serpentine.

It took him about five minutes to reach the lake's edge and another minute before he discovered a suitable place to lay down his burden. When he had done so he felt in his pocket for his handkerchief and, having found it, dipped it in the water, wrung it out, and applied it in the form of a cold compress to the Professor's forehead. While he was doing this he became aware that he was no longer alone. A number of dark shapes had crept out of the undergrowth and had gathered round him in a sinister, watchful, semicircle.

– 'What you got there, monkey?'
– 'Got you a pinkie, have you?'
– 'Where d'you get her, monkey?'
– 'Still warm ain't she?'

Listening to the whispered questions Norbert felt the hair rise along the back of his neck. He guessed from their speech that these were what were known as 'bad apes' – chimps who had dropped out and now lived an illegal sort of twilight existence on the fringes of civilized society. Among them the insulting epithet 'monkey' was a veritable badge of kinship, signifying the brotherhood of the lower depths.

'She's sick,' he grunted dabbing the wet cloth across the Professor's deathly brow.

'Who ain't?' came the laconic retort.

A sinewy arm stretched out from the darkness and a hairy hand descended speculatively on Professor Poynter's flat chest. Norbert knocked it aside and flashed his teeth in a rage warning. The shadows skipped back a wary pace and squatted down. The whispered questions began again.

– 'Where d'you get her, monkey?'
– 'Anyone see you?'
– 'Where you from, monkey?'
– 'Reckon he's an Albert?'

This last remark was a reference to a chimp who, back in the 1990s, had gained a (Posthumous) Congressional Medal for sacrificing his life to save those of three human companions in a space-craft disaster. To these drop-outs it symbolized the ultimate in 'Uncle Tom'-ism.

'We were in that march,' grunted Norbert.

'So what?'

'So that makes me an Albert?'

'Don't give us that V.F.A. shit, monkey.'

'Hey, what happened in there?' enquired a different, younger voice.

'You don't know?'

'Some sort of shindy?'

'Shindy!' Norbert spat. 'A massacre. Only two of us got out alive.'

'You and her?'

'That's right.'

'Hey, whatja know? 'S that what all the excitement's about?'

Under his hand Norbert felt Professor Poynter stir. He prayed that she wouldn't give the game away.

The shadows were whispering again but this time with a different purpose and a new sense of urgency.

– 'There has to be pickings.'

– 'We can do a drop. They won't skin the trees.'

– 'What's the screw on, monkey?'

'There are Guards round the edges,' said Norbert. 'Not more than a couple of dozen.'

– 'What're we waiting for?'

A sudden scuffling in the undergrowth and they were gone.

Norbert let out his breath in a protracted sigh and felt the bristling hair along his neck slowly settle. 'Come on, ma'am,' he whispered. 'It's not safe for us to stay here.'

Professor Poynter's teeth chattered like shaken pebbles. He slid his arm beneath her quivering shoulder and coaxed her up into a sitting position. 'Can you walk, ma'am?'

'Mad,' shuddered the Professor. 'Stark, raving mad!'

'We can't stay here, ma'am.'

'Cold blooded mass murder! Insane! Absolutely and utterly insane!'

'Ma'am.'

'Adrenal hypertension ... breakthrough ... augmented adrenal hypertension ... sound principle ... all mad ... mad ... arms ... legs and arms ...' Her voice broke into a harsh dry sobbing.

Norbert hooked one of her arms round his neck and stood up, pulling her with him. 'Where d'you live, ma'am?'

'So much blood and pain,' sobbed the Professor. 'Just because it's *legal* doesn't give them the *moral* right ...'

Norbert shook her gently and repeated his question more urgently.

'Richmond,' gasped the Professor. 'Kew Mansions, Richmond.'

The chimp looked round at the horizon, now pin-pricked with a million hazy apartment lights. Behind him the *Minisoc* floodlights seemed to have blown a bubble of greenish light among the trees. To the south a crimson sky sign smouldered out the message: *SUBURBAN EXPRESSWAY*. 'Come on, ma'am,' he said gently. 'Let's try our luck over there.'

13

CHERYL UNBUCKLED HER A-G harness and hung it in the closet alongside her bag of assorted oblivions. Then she washed her hands, gave her hair a perfunctory scrub with a perfumed flexibrush and returned to the living room. 'Oh, are you still here?' she said, affecting surprise at the sight of Alvin's beaming face. 'The front door's down there.'

'Could I use your toilet, please?'

'Oh *anything*,' sighed Cheryl. 'Just make yourself at home.'

'Thanks,' said the clone fervently. 'Where is it?'

'Second on the right.'

She watched him poke his nose round the door of the ablution cubicle before disappearing inside. Shaking her head in mock despair she walked over to the videophone and dialled a number. A plump avuncular face loomed up in the screen. 'Ah, there y'are, Cheryl! Mission completed?'

She nodded.

'Well done, lass. It's time for your break now anyway.'

'Do you know what's been going on down at Speakers' Corner, Dommy?'

'Did ye not see "*Your Day*"?'

'How could I? My set's been dead for the last fortnight.'

'A couple of lots of protestors went for each others' throats. Quite a pitched battle, I can tell ye.'

'But why should they do that?'

'Why indeed? The whisper has it that *Minisoc* were behind it.'

'Were they?'

'It wouldn't surprise me, and that's the truth. Was that where your call was?'

'Oh no,' said Cheryl hastily. 'It was just that I noticed a lot of activity down there. Thanks anyway, Dommy.'

'A pleasure, my love. I'll be slottin' you in for the 24 to 2 rush. O.K.?'

Cheryl nodded and smiled then thumbed the 'line clear' button. As the glow faded from the screen she tried to reconcile what Dominic had told her with her visual recollection of the heaps of mangled corpses scattered under the trees. However hard she tried to push them together the two pictures just wouldn't fuse. She was still pondering on it when Alvin emerged from the toilet, glanced shyly in at her and shuffled hesitantly into the room. Cheryl regarded him thoughtfully. 'Tell me, Alvin, just what *did* happen down there in the Park?'

Alvin scratched his ear and frowned. 'I don't know,' he admitted.

'But you must know *something*!'

'Well, only what I told you.'

'But how did you come to be mixed up in it? You're not a recalcitrant, are you?'

Alvin didn't know whether he was or not, so he compromised by describing as much as he could remember of what had happened from the moment Norbert and he had left Aldbury.

Cheryl listened attentively. When he had finished she said: 'Then why did you tell me you were staying in Bristol Street?'

Alvin looked down at his boots and felt his ears turning a hot, bright pink. 'I just didn't want to lose you,' he mumbled.

She remembered something else. 'And you said you'd seen me yesterday! That was another lie, wasn't it?'

'Oh *no*!' cried Alvin. 'I *did* see you! I *did*! Only it wasn't like it was when it happened. I thought you must have been someone from Before. But you can't be, can you?'

Even though Cheryl had no idea what he was talking about, the sheer intensity of his denial made a tiny shiver run all the way up and down her backbone.

The clone looked wonderingly into her face and then slowly raised his eyes until he appeared to be contemplating a point somewhere in the air above her left shoulder. 'You were sort of bending over me,' he murmured. 'And you were smiling.'

For no reason at all Cheryl shivered again. 'You really are a nut, Alvin,' she said.

'But it *will* happen!' he insisted. 'One day it will.'

'That'll be the day,' she grunted. 'Now hadn't you better trot along and find out what's happened to your chimp friend?'

'Oh my goodness!' cried Alvin. 'He'll be terribly worried. He's meant to be looking after me.'

'You're sure it isn't the other way round?' she observed wryly. 'He doesn't seem to be doing much of a job so far.'

'But that wasn't his fault,' said Alvin stoutly. 'I think he must have been hit on the head or something. He didn't seem to remember where we were supposed to be going.'

'Well, why didn't you remind him then?'

Again Alvin blushed. 'I don't know,' he muttered.

'Don't you?' murmured Cheryl. 'Really?'

Something most peculiar was happening to Alvin's knees, causing his legs to behave rather like a pair of warm wax candles. He would in all probability have subsided on to the carpet at her feet had he not been suddenly petrified by an eidetic vision of Doctor Pfizier at his most censorious. 'Norbert!' he gulped.

As though lit inwardly by tiny emerald flames, Cheryl's eyes twinkled mischievously. 'What about Norbert?'

'Must go and find him. Must, musn't I?'

For a long, long moment she appeared to consider this, then she sighed faintly. 'All right,' she said. 'Come on, I'll take you down. I've got to do some shopping anyway.'

She disappeared into the closet to emerge, a moment later, wearing a dark green cape and hood. She looked so utterly delectable that Alvin was temporarily bereft of speech. Before he could recover the use of his tongue she had steered him out of the apartment and slammed the door firmly behind them.

14

BRISTOL STREET WAS not a modern residential development. It had been built in the early years of the 21st century at least a decade before the invention of 'skylighting' had ushered in the gargantuan 'Tower' units which now dominated London. Its two hundred modest storeys were a mere four apartments wide and its lateral stability was derived from the intricate system of pedestrian-interlink hollow buttresses which connected it to Mount Street on one side and Alford Street on the other. Cheryl had once compared them to three long thin slices of mouldy bread skewered together by aluminium knitting needles – a simile which, though fanciful, had considerable visual accuracy.

Her own balcony apartment was on the 174th floor and her immediate neighbours were a masseuse, a Dream Palace transvestite, two free-lance Authenticity Spectators, and a small time professional gambler. She knew them all, but was on really friendly terms only with Joe and Chrissie the two So-Vi Spectators. On several occasions, clutching a forged A.S. union card and tricked out in a blonde wig and dark glasses, she had accompanied them to the London stadiums. There at the bidding of the Crowd Director she had whirled a rattle and screamed till she was red in the face while the teams of brilliantly-shirted footballers performed their ritual skills in the remote arena far below.

The knowledge that she was breaking the law by impersonating a union member never caused her even a momentary qualm. On the contrary it constituted a major element of her pleasure, for it produced in her the delicious epidermal tingling which she had long ago found she needed almost as much as other less fortunate people needed her deadly toxins. This was the appetite which she had been indulging when she had twitched Alvin from under the nose of *Minisoc*. One day, no doubt, she would go too far, but until that happened she had every intention of continuing as she had begun, appeasing her hunger for excitement whenever she felt the urge to do so.

The truth of the matter is that Cheryl, like so many millions of others before her, was still trying to discover who she really was. It was not that she had any particular ambition to re-bake the social cake, but she did want to discover the particular slice of it that she was certain was meant for her alone. So she nibbled around wherever the opportunity presented itself and, as a result her short past was already littered with the crumbs of a surprising variety of experiences, which, had she chosen to talk of them, would certainly have astounded her parents.

At this moment, steering Alvin down the passage towards the elevator rank, she found herself wondering just what it was about him that had so far prevented her from simply shooing him out of her life like any other stray biped. True he was the first of his particular species that she had encountered, but since she had no knowledge of his genetic peculiarities, this could hardly be said to count. Yet undoubtedly there was something there that intrigued her. Even when she wasn't actually *looking* at him she couldn't help being *aware* of him. He was like some fiddling little task which you go on putting off while, at the back of your mind, is the nagging realization that one day it will have to be attended to. Yes, she decided, he was a sort of spiritual loose thread who would be for ever catching on her until finally she would be compelled either to snip him off or darn him in. 'What's your other name, Alvin?' she asked.

'I haven't got one.'

'Why not? I thought only apes had one name.'

Alvin squirmed under her scrutiny. 'Doctor Pfizier never gave me one.'

'And who's Doctor Pfizier?'

'My god-father.'

'Then who's your real father?'

'I don't know,' said Alvin. 'I don't think Doctor Pfizier is.'

Cheryl eyed him curiously. 'You mean he adopted you?'

'I suppose he must have done.'

'Don't you *know*?'

'Well, you see, I only remember from Aldbury,' explained Alvin uncomfortably.

Cheryl glanced up at the elevator indicator and saw one of the lights change from 198 to 195. She walked to the appropriate control and pushed the button. 'No, I don't see,' she said.

Alvin's face went bright pink and he scrubbed his straw-coloured hair furiously. 'Well, before that – was, well . . . *Before*,' he explained in a throttled sort of voice.

'Before *what*?' persisted Cheryl.

Alvin made a choking noise. 'Before I *was*,' he gulped.

'That's crazy,' said Cheryl. 'You weren't *born* there, were you?'

'No,' said Alvin.

'Well then?'

'Doctor Pfizier said I wouldn't remember anything from Before,' said Alvin. 'He said if I did it would mean there was something wrong with me.'

'He sounds a pretty sinister sort of creep to me,' said Cheryl. 'Come on, here's ours.'

'Oh no, he's not,' protested Alvin, following her into the pressurized elevator capsule. 'He's good. Really good.'

'How do you know he is?' said Cheryl, sealing the doors and setting the lift plummeting groundwards. 'He told you so, I suppose?'

'Yes,' said Alvin simply. 'Often.'

'And if I told you I was good, you'd swallow that too, I suppose?'

'Of course you are,' said Alvin. 'I know you didn't mean that about wanting to kill me.'

'I didn't, huh?' nodded Cheryl. 'No doubt you think Samaritans are paid by the government to go round saving people's lives.'

Alvin laughed. His laughter had always been one of his most endearing features and Cheryl found it remarkably infectious. 'You're out of this world, Alvin!' she cried. 'You really are!'

They were still giggling when the elevator began to slow, thrusting them down into the grubby horse-shoe shaped foam couch. 'Hey!' gasped the clone. 'What's going on?'

'I suppose you're going to tell me you've never been in an expressavator before.'

Alvin shook his head and wondered where his stomach had gone. 'I haven't,' he said. 'They only have ordinary lifts at Aldbury.'

Cheryl stood up, unsealed the doors, then pulled the clone to his feet and led him out of the vestibule into the thronged service area. 'Our flow-way's been out of action all week,' she said. 'It's always going wrong. But it's only about five minutes' walk from here.'

She guided him down the crowded alleyway to the brightly lit arcade whose shops supplied the everyday needs of the denizens of Bristol Street and they emerged, a few minutes later, in Park Lane. 'Well, there you are,' she said. 'That's the Park straight ahead.'

Alvin looked at her in dismay. 'Aren't you coming with me?'

Cheryl eyed him pensively. To snip or not to snip, that was the question. 'You don't need my help,' she said.

'But what if he's not there?'

'Why shouldn't he be?'

'Please come, Cheryl.'

She held her mental scissors poised. One swift clip and the job would be done.

'*Please*, Cheryl.'

'Oh, all *right*,' she said grudgingly. 'There's a gate up there.'

There was no traffic for them to bother about. Apart from Government vehicles, all urban transport had long since been either buried underground or trellised high in the air. The ten-lane freeways which had once so nearly strangled the cities to death had vanished along with their infernal freight, their passing lamented only by those statisticians who mourned a magnificent contribution to the monthly mortality figures. Where once pedestrians had gone in fear of their lives there was now little more to be heard than the sound of human and anthropoid voices, punctuated by the brisk *cloppity-clop* of a Security prancer or the benevolent hiss of A-G jets as some public servant whistled across the City.

Even so there were still many areas of the vast metropolis where the average citizen was careful not to venture after sundown and where the Guards went in twos or threes if they went at all. After dark safety lay with the crowd and the brightly lit precinct. So it was not simply reluctance to involve herself further with Alvin that had caused Cheryl to hesitate, but an instinctive disinclination to attract the attentions of the Nightpeople.

However, as the officials were obviously still working at the scene of the Protest Massacre, Cheryl reasoned that, with all the activity going on she and Alvin would surely be safe. So keeping a wary eye on the shadows she stepped through the gateway and, grasping the clone firmly by the arm, hurried him over the damp grass towards the *Minisoc* floodlights.

15

As ALVIN AND Cheryl re-entered the Park, Norbert and Professor Poynter were just leaving it via an escalator which was bearing them aloft to the Kensington Expressway platforms. By an incredible fluke of which they were both unaware, they had encountered neither ape nor human in their trek from the Serpentine. Had they done so the chances were that their journey would have ended there and then.

Norbert discovered that a train calling at Richmond was expected to depart on the southern circuit within the next quarter of an hour. He turned to Professor Poynter and asked her whether she thought she would be able to manage on her own.

'You have been most kind,' she murmured. 'Most kind.'

'Not at all, ma'am,' responded Norbert modestly. 'Did not the Good Lord say that we must help one another in times of trial and tribulation?'

'Trial and tribulation, yes,' nodded the Professor. 'A religious faith must be a great standby at such times.'

'At *all* times, ma'am. His ministers are everywhere about us. Why, only a matter of minutes before we met, my young companion Alvin was carried up to Heaven by an angel, and I too was privileged to enjoy a somewhat shorter flight.'

Professor Poynter passed her hand across her brow. 'Forgive me,' she murmured. 'I thought for one moment that you said "Alvin".'

'Indeed, I did, ma'am. And what sweeter, purer lad e'er drew breath? Wherever he may be I shall always think of young Alvin as the flower of Aldbury.'

Professor Poynter's hands reached out and clutched the ape by the wrist. 'Did you say "Aldbury"? Aldbury near Aylesbury?'

'Why, yes, ma'am. Do you know it?'

'You come from there?'

'Indeed I do.'

'And this lad – Alvin – would he be moon-faced? with prominent ears? and pale blue eyes? and hair like straw?'

Norbert smiled delightedly. 'Why, you have drawn his portrait to the life, ma'am! But how is this possible?'

'Of *course*!' cried the Professor. '*Norbert!* How incredibly obtuse of me! Doctor Pfizier said you were bringing him to London! Do you mean to tell me he *wasn't* killed? That he's *survived*? Oh Norbert! Norbert! Can this be true?'

A tear moistened Norbert's kindly eye. 'Ma'am,' he explained sorrowfully, 'I fear that my recent unhappy experiences have impaired my memory. I recollect very well that Alvin and I left Aldbury this morning, but the purpose of our journey, alas, escapes me. Shortly before he was translated Heavenwards he informed me that we were here on holiday, and knowing the lad to be incapable of uttering a falsehood I can only conclude that such is indeed the case.'

Professor Poynter was now trembling as violently with excitement as, previously, she had trembled from shock. 'This angel you speak of,' she said. 'Can you describe it?'

'It was a she-angel,' said Norbert, 'and surpassingly comely to behold. About five foot four and slender as a peeled willow wand. Her wings might well have resembled those of the lesser hover-fly; I recall that they made a distinct hissing noise. She informed us her name was Cheryl.'

'Cheryl?'

'Yes,' said Norbert. 'A name almost as beautiful as the fair creature who bore it.'

'Did she have a belt?'

'A girdle of the purest silver encircled her slender waist – with shoulder straps to match.'

'But how did she find you?'

'Unworthy though I am she came in answer to my prayers,' said Norbert simply. 'Not a sparrow falls but they know about it up there.'

'Then you didn't – well, *phone* or anything?'

'God's videophone, ma'am,' replied Norbert gently, 'is the pure and humble heart.'

The faint undertone of reproof in his words warmed Professor Poynter's numbed soul like a mouthful of Five Star Eroticon. In full view of several hundred shocked or amused travellers she raised the ape's lined pink hand in both of hers and pressed it to her lips. 'Oh Norbert,' she murmured brokenly, 'I believe *you* are an angel.'

'Alas, no, ma'am,' he replied. 'But it's good of you to say so.'

'I *do* say so,' affirmed Professor Poynter. 'Oh Norbert, my dear, you have restored my faith in natural goodness. Together we will battle against the forces of evil that are abroad in the land! Together we shall overcome them! Say you are with me, Norbert!'

Always quick to respond to sincerity, Norbert was deeply touched by the appeal. Taking her hands solemnly into his he shook them warmly. 'I only wish you could have met Alvin, ma'am,' he sighed. 'You and he would have got along like a house on fire.'

'But I *have* met him!' she laughed. 'I'm Professor Poynter! You were bringing him to see me at the M.O.P.'

Norbert blinked. 'Why, *yes*,' he murmured slowly. 'I remember now. The M.O.P. . . . . I've got all the papers . . .' He looked round vaguely for his brief-case then frowned and rubbed his wrinkled forehead. 'Balls,' he whispered wonderingly, 'balls, balls, we want balls.'

'I'm sorry,' said Professor Poynter. 'I didn't quite . . .'

'We were in a march, ma'am,' said Norbert hesitantly. 'Alvin and me. We were trying to get to Croydon. And then . . . and then, the next thing I recall is the lad giving me a drink of water out of a boot and all around us more dead bodies than when Samson fell upon the Philistines.'

Professor Poynter shuddered with sudden violence. 'I know,' she said. 'It is a miracle you both survived.'

'Did you come to look for us, ma'am?'

She nodded. 'By sheer chance I happened to see Alvin's face on the So-Vi screen this evening. I went along to try to find him. The experience proved rather more than I could take. At which point, I'm afraid, my own recollection becomes a little hazy.'

A train slid into the station beside them and its doors purred open. 'Come along, Norbert, my dear,' said the Professor. 'We two have much to learn from one another.'

'Thank you, ma'am,' said the chimp and stepped beside her into the compartment.

16

ONE OF THE Security Guards caught sight of Alvin and Cheryl approaching and warned them to clear off if they knew what was good for them.

'We're looking for a friend,' explained Alvin politely.

'Try the Kennington Morgue between 9 and 12 tomorrow morning. Now hop it!'

Alvin had started to say 'Oh, but he isn't d—' when Cheryl's sharp tug on his arm spun him round on his heel.

She jerked her head in the direction of the laurel clump where she had deposited Norbert. 'Come on,' she hissed. 'We'll walk towards it and whisper to him to get out on the other side.'

'What if he's not there?'

'That's your worry, not mine.'

'Don't you like apes, Cheryl?'

'Apes are fine,' she muttered. 'But right now all I'm interested in is getting out of this spooky Park.'

'I know more apes than I know people,' said Alvin chattily.

'They're great, Cheryl, really they are. All my best friends are apes. Except you and Doctor Pfizier, that is.'

'I'm flattered,' she grunted. 'Let's hope they've taught you a few useful passwords.'

'What do you mean?'

'Well, by all accounts there are some pretty peculiar specimens around this part of the world. If those Security mushrooms hadn't been within shouting range you'd never have got me in here conscious after dark. Not on foot, anyway.'

'But an ape wouldn't touch a hair on your head, Cheryl. They're good and kind, really they are.'

'Maybe they are where you come from. Here I wouldn't count on it.'

By this time they had approached within a few yards of the shrubbery. 'Norbert?' called Alvin softly. 'Norbert, it's us.'

There was no answer. He took a pace nearer and tried again. This time he thought he detected some faint sounds in the undergrowth – the tiny crack of a breaking twiglet; the soft hush of pent breath being slowly expelled. 'Norbert!' he whispered as loudly as he dared. 'You can come out now. Round the back so no one'll see you.'

This time the response was unequivocal. An answering grunt of affirmation and the noise of a body thrusting its way through the bushes. 'He's going round,' whispered Alvin. 'Come on.'

He trotted ahead into the shadows. Cheryl had taken three paces after him when some sixth sense made her pause. 'Alvin,' she whispered fearfully. 'Are you –'

The rest of the sentence never materialized. A section of shadow slipped from the shrubbery beside her; a gloved hand clamped itself expertly across her mouth and nose, and she was bundled backwards into the bushes as unceremoniously as washing is snatched from a line at the approach of rain.

Alvin meanwhile had received even shorter shrift. A sandbag having landed smartly behind his left ear, he had just taken a precipitate nosedive into the dark waters of unconsciousness for the second time in six hours.

He came to some thirty minutes later when a large water drop, which had percolated through the concrete roof of the disused underground garage where he was lying, gathered itself together and dropped plumb on to his left eyelid. He groaned piteously, thereby attracting the attention of an ancient female chimp who was squatting in the front seat of a ruined Chevrolet, picking cigar butts to pieces and dropping the fragrant chaff into a sawn-off plastic jerrycan. As Alvin attempted to roll over she stuck out her foot and pushed him back again. 'Lie still, pinkie,' she said, 'an' be a good boy.'

To Alvin who to the best of his knowledge had never been anything else, this did not present much difficulty since he was trussed hand and foot and his head was pounding like a police-man's boots. He blinked the water out of his eye and peered groggily up at the lichened concrete above him. 'Where am I?' he demanded weakly.

'Why, you're right here, son, that's where,' cackled the simian gargoyle obviously delighted by her own wit.

'Is Cheryl here too?'

'She the little pussy they brought in alonger you?'

'Where is she?'

'Don't you worry, son. She's being well looked after. A right sensible gel. Pretty too. Surprised a bright lad like you took her strollin' in the Park after dark.'

'We were looking for a friend.'

'Were you now?' said the crone, selecting a two-inch stub of a *Romeo-y-Julietta* and cracking it with a gnarled thumb. 'Just fancy that!'

'Is he here too?'

'And who might "he" be?'

Alvin sniffed tearfully. 'Norbert,' he said. 'An ape.'

'We don't keep no Alberts, son. They're not tradeable, see?'

'Treadeable?'

'Sure. What did you think? We was a-goin' t' *eat* yer?' She sniggered ghoulishly and poked him in the ribs with a bony prehensile toe. 'Not that I'd say no ter a bitty nibble. Come t'think on't I ain't tasted me a pinkie since I was a gel truckin' in Mater-nity.'

At that moment it occurred to Alvin that he was being punished for all those wicked lies he had told Norbert and Cheryl, the two people he loved most in the whole world apart from Doctor Pfizier. He began to cry in real earnest.

'Now what's the good of that?' grumbled the crone. 'This place is damp enough already without you mekkin' it worse. Give over now there's a good lad.'

Before Alvin had time to respond there was a reverberant metallic crash, followed, a moment later by the clatter of boots and the shouted query: 'He round yet, Maggie?'

'Yep,' chirped the crone. 'He's all yours, boys. An' welcome to him.'

Two young male apes, uniformed in black dungarees and black berets, and with lasers slung across their backs, stooped over the blubbering Alvin and slashed through the flex that was binding his ankles. Then they hoisted him to his feet and propelled him down the passage by a hand gripped above each of his elbows.

They marched him through various echoing vaults in which the carcasses of ancient automobiles were crumbling silently into rust and brought him eventually to a metal door on which a rough sign of two clasped hands had been daubed in yellow paint. One of the apes rapped three times with the butt of his laser then paused and knocked three times more. At this there was a scraping of bolts from within, the door was dragged to one side, and Alvin was thrust forward into the room.

Blinking through his tear-swollen eyes he saw before him a metal desk behind which a thick-set, middle-aged chimp in black horn-rimmed spectacles was bent writing something in a notebook. On the wall behind the desk were fixed two crude but arresting posters, one proclaiming *The Dictatorship of the Proletariape is at Hand!* and the other *Universal Anthropoid Brotherhood!* In one corner stood a metal cabinet and in another a So-Vi. Some metal chairs were ranged along a wall and one was placed directly before the desk. The spectacled ape glanced up, nodded towards this chair, and then returned his attention to his notebook. The young ape who had opened the door untied the flex from Alvin's wrists and then thrust him forward into the seat.

For a long time nothing more happened. Alvin sniffed despondently and wiped his dripping nose surreptitiously on his sleeve. He had no idea why he was there or what was meant by the dictatorship of the proletariape, but he quite liked the two posters. The first depicted an endless line of laughing chimps striding out

74

under a huge banner on which was emblazoned the sign of the clasped hands and the initials '*U.A.B*'; the second portrayed two anthropoids, one shouldering a laser gun and the other wielding a spanner, embracing over the command '*Monkeys Unite!*'

At least the ape finished writing and read through what he had written. After altering a couple of words here and there he tore out the page and handed it to the chimp who was guarding the door. Then he laid down his pen, unhooked his spectacles and massaged the bridge of his nose. Behind Alvin the door opened and closed again. Finally the ape replaced his spectacles and contemplated the clone curiously.

Alvin felt himself beginning to blush and looked down shyly at the soles of the ape's boots which were protruding beneath the desk. He felt as he often felt when he was summoned to Doctor Pfizier's office – that is to say guilty without being quite sure what he should be feeling guilty about.

'Well,' said the ape at last, 'and who the hell are you?'

'Alvin, sir.'

The ape blinked. 'We'll cut out the decadent lackey lip for a start,' he growled. 'Call me Captain, comrade. At least that doesn't stink of serfdom.'

'Yes, Captain Comrade, sir. I mean no.'

The ape appeared to emit something that sounded suspiciously like a sigh. He picked up his pen. 'Political affiliation?' he demanded.

Alvin looked supremely blank.

'Who did you vote for last time?'

A faint gleam of something that might almost have passed for intelligence flickered like a December sunbeam across the clone's face. 'Oh, Norbert, of course,' he said.

'Huh?'

'Norbert,' repeated Alvin. 'He beat Bosun by seventeen.'

The ape laid down his pen then picked it up again. He examined it carefully for a while and breathed heavily through his nose. 'And who, or what, is Norbert?' he enquired.

'He's our branch leader of the A.S.T.W.'

'What do you mean *your* branch leader?'

'It's my union,' said Alvin. 'Here's my card.' He reached into his breast and discovered that his pockets were empty.

'Would this be what you're looking for?' said the ape. He pulled open a drawer and lifted from it a few documents and some currency notes. From the pile he selected a rectangle of green plasticard. 'Anthropoid Scientific and Technical Workers' Union,' he read out. 'Aldbury Branch. Member's Name: Alvin. Membership Number: 7663251. Trade: General Worker. Grade: D.'

'Yes,' said Alvin proudly. 'That's it.'

'How did you get hold of this?'

Alvin blinked. 'It's mine,' he said.

The Captain nodded with ponderous irony. 'And you, no doubt, are a renegade anthropoid cunningly disguised as a human idiot.'

Alvin blushed. 'I'm an honorary ape, Captain Comrade. It was Norbert's idea.'

The Captain opened his mouth and then closed it again without saying anything. He placed his elbows on the desk, shaded his eyes with his palms and appeared to be thinking very, very deeply. In fact he was undergoing the chastening experience of having to admit to himself that this moonfaced oaf fitted into no category he had previously encountered in a life-time dedicated to the struggles of the proletariape.

To gain himself a little time he rolled a cigarette, lit it, and inhaled deeply. The scent of second-hand Havana leaf floated across the desk. 'You realize, of course,' he said, 'that I should be doing no more than my political duty if I had you liquidated on a charge of species impersonation.'

Perhaps fortunately, Alvin did not know what he meant. He continued to blink amiably through the layers of violet smoke while he wondered where Cheryl was.

'We have no need of any honorary apes in our ranks,' growled the Captain. 'The mere idea is an affront to anthropoid integrity, a sneaky undermining of species solidarity.' So saying he picked up Alvin's Union card and flicked it across the room towards an overflowing wastepaper basket.

Alvin watched it flutter down and wondered why the Comrade Captain seemed so offended. He himself was not particularly upset since he was always losing his card and having to ask Norbert for a new one.

'Ape is Ape,' continued the Captain, 'and Man is Man. The struggle for species equality will be won only when the last man has been forced to acknowledge the social existence of the last anthropoid. Until that day no quarter will be asked or given. Our resolution has been fired in the furnace of injustice; forged on the anvil of slavery and tempered in the acid-bath of exploitation! The species struggle is the war of the oppressed against the oppressor – of the slave against his bondage; but, above all, today, it is the struggle of the ape against *himself*! To *be* free an ape must *think* free! He must learn to believe in his heritage! And to do that he must be prepared to die for it!'

Alvin nodded. Although he had not understood half of it, the Captain's words had stirred him deeply. 'Nearly all my best friends are apes,' he said amicably.

The Captain grunted. 'Intra-special companionship is a poisonous delusion fostered by our enemies. True comradeship is only possible between equals.'

'They *are* much cleverer than I am,' admitted Alvin, 'but honestly they don't seem to mind that. Except Bosun,' he added regretfully.

The Captain picked up his pen again, wrote something in his notebook, then changed his mind and scribbled it out. Try as he would he was finding it quite impossible to come to terms with Alvin. Like the dying King Arthur he found that 'all his Mind was clouded with a Doubt'. It seemed almost incredible to him that anyone so stupid could have survived for so long in the world. If this was what the oppressors had come to then the day of revolution must be considerably closer than anyone could have supposed. He suspected, unfortunately, that not only was Alvin distinctly atypical, but that no one in his right mind would pay a plastic cent to ransom him. Still, one could but try. 'Who's your father, lad?' he asked.

'I don't know, Captain Comrade.'

'Well, who do you – belong to?'

'Doctor Pfizier, I suppose.'

'And how do we get in touch with him?'

'He's at Aldbury,' said Alvin. 'He's in charge there.'

'And where's Aldbury?'

Alvin explained as best he could.

The Captain sighed. 'It's worth a try. How much d'you think he'd fork out to get you back again?'

Alvin gasped. 'Pay?' he gulped. 'For *me*?'

'That's right.'

Alvin's eye roved round the room as though he were expecting to find the magic figure suddenly written on one of the walls. 'I don't suppose he'd pay anything,' he said sadly. 'You see, I pay him.'

'Come again?'

'I pay him half my wages each month for teaching me.'

'Teaching you what?'

'How to be good,' said Alvin.

'*How to be good?*' repeated the Captain in a stunned voice.

Alvin nodded. 'Doctor Pfizier says they're the toughest hundreds he's ever earned in his life.'

The Captain laid down his pen and stared long and incredulously at the unhappy clone. Finally he stubbed out his cigarette, pushed back his chair, and walked slowly across the room to the wastepaper basket. Bending down he retrieved Alvin's union card. He wiped it on his sleeve, peered at it closely, and then handed it back to Alvin. 'Take it, son,' he said. 'It's yours all right. Only a bloody monkey would put up with that sort of exploitation.'

'Oh thank you, Captain Comrade,' said Alvin, accepting the card gratefully. 'Can I go to Cheryl now?'

The Captain shrugged. 'You're no use to us. We shall release you.'

'But Captain Com –'

'You would prefer to be liquidated?'

'Oh, please don't send me away,' begged Alvin. 'Not without Cheryl! Please, *please*, dear kind Captain Comrade!'

'What is she to you?' growled the Captain, regarding the oaf with mingled pity and distaste.

Like dilute cochineal across a filter paper, an expression of refulgent imbecility crept across Alvin's face. 'Oh Captain Comrade,' he sighed rapturously. 'Cheryl is the starlight trembling on Lake Tring on summer evenings! She is crunchy peanut butter on warm toast! She is an angel!'

'She is a female hireling of an effete and decadent technocracy,' retorted the Captain. 'An arch-enemy of the proletariape. What's more she's skinny too.'

'I love her,' said Alvin simply.

'You, my friend, are an idiot.'

'I know,' said Alvin. 'Doctor Pfizier's told me so lots of times.'

'Furthermore you have no self-respect, no financial value, and absolutely no political value! You belong in a zoo!'

'He's told me that too,' admitted Alvin dejectedly.

'However, by allowing you to go free we shall perhaps advance the cause of the species struggle by an infinitesimal degree. It is just conceivable that you will contrive to breed more idiots like yourself. Though how you will persuade anyone to help you do it defies my imagination.' He walked to the door, dragged it open and grunted something to the guards outside. Then he turned back to Alvin. 'I will decide later what is to be done with you.'

'Oh, *thank you*, Captain Comrade sir,' beamed Alvin. 'As soon as I saw you I knew you were good and kind.'

'Just take him away,' groaned the Captain. 'And tell Maggie to bring me some strong black coffee.'

17

NORBERT AND PROFESSOR Poynter reached Kew Mansions, Richmond shortly after midnight. Although they did not know it their approach was observed and noted by a MOSS agent, an anthropoid named Pinkerton, known professionally to his employers as '0726'. For the last hour, ever since the green security alert had gone out from the Censorship Vaults, this character had been hanging around the expressavator vestibule of Kew Mansions disguised as a So-Vi technician. Having ascertained from an irritable Hortense that the Professor was out, Pinkerton had decided that his employers' ends would best be served by awaiting her return and then manufacturing an opportunity to plant an eavesdropper on her.

In the event this proved a simple enough operation because Norbert and the Professor were in such deep conversation that they paid not the slightest attention to the overalled artisan who touched his cap and squeezed into the expressavator capsule alongside them. Pinkerton was able to tag them with two bugs apiece and would no doubt have added a third if he could have thought of somewhere useful to put it. These ingenious gadgets which were self-adhesive and scarcely larger than a piece of confetti had an effective transmission range of nearly two miles and could monitor speech within a radius of up to ten metres. Since they were virtually indestructible, those who discovered them and recognized what they were, usually got rid of them by flushing them down the toilet or, occasionally, by transferring them surreptitiously to some unsuspecting stranger – a practice which MOSS considered most unsporting.

Having planted his bugs Pinkerton left the expressavator, returned to ground level and hurried to the nearest MOSS monitoring post which was cunningly concealed in the back of a nearby laundrette. Here, a few moments later, he recorded the following conversation –

– Are you awake, petal?
– Where the helluv you *been*?
– I'll tell you all about it tomorrow.
– D'you find him?
– Well, no, not exactly, but –
– Then who the hell's that moving around in –
– That's Norbert.
– Norbert who?
– It's too late to explain now, petal. You go back to sleep again.
– I haven't *been* to sleep. I was just dropping off when some moronic monkey came and –
– I do wish you wouldn't use that expression, petal. It's so de*grad*ing.
– What're you whispering for?
– Would you like me to switch on your Henry?
– Aren't you coming to bed then?

– Not just now. I've got to talk to Norbert.

– Who the hell *is* this Norbert?

– He's a friend, petal. A very dear friend.

– Since when? It's the first I've heard of him.

– He saved my life tonight.

– You don't say? Well, let's have a look at him. Hey there, Norbert!

– Ma'am?

– Petal, I . . . Do put something on, my sweet!

– Is he *shy*, or something? Come right on in, Norbert. Let's have a look at you.

– Petal, sweetest, I don't –

– Ma'am? Did you –

– Oh *no*! AH-H-H-h-h-h . . . ! ! !

– Oh, dear, ma'am! Has she fainted?

– It's my fault. Norbert. I should have realized. Hortense had a most unfortunate experience when she was a child, and as a result . . .

– I understand, ma'am. I'm truly sorry. Is there anything I can do to help?

– I don't think so, Norbert. But perhaps it *would* be better if . . .

– Of course, ma'am. I'll wait in the other room.

– There, there, petal. It's quite all right. There, there . . .

– *Oooh . . . gggh . . . ugg . . . ggg . . .*

– There's absolutely nothing at all to be upset about. Here, drink this, my sweet.

– *Glug . . . gh . . . uh . . . glup . . .*

– That's better. There, there . . .

– Has it gone?

– Yes, yes.

– It was horrible – *horrible*! How *could* you!

– Now, there's no need to get hysterical.

– *Hysterical!* You can say that! You don't know what it's like to have to lie there and have one after another of those . . . *six* of them there were . . . *six* . . .

– That was a long time ago, my sweet. And besides it never was six. You know we settled all that. There was only one, and he . . .

– It *was* six! It *was*! Six great black hairy ... One after the other.

– Now, petal, it's no good your going on like ...

– It didn't happen to you!

– No, my pet.

– Well, then.

– Now listen, my darlingest, you really must try to understand that, morally speaking, apes are no different from the rest of us. There are as many good ones as bad ones. Norbert is far more profoundly Christian than some of the twisted individuals who have the audacity to call themselves human. He risked his own life for me tonight without a moment's hesitation and I have –

– Monkey lover!

– There's a very hard streak in you, Hortense. I've noticed it before. Now I fully realize that you're upset and so I intend to overlook –

– Monkey lover! Monkey lover!

– I'm sorry, Hortense, there is obviously no point in our discussing the matter further. I shall be next door if you want me. Goodnight.

– Is she feeling better, ma'am?

– Yes, thank you, Norbert. Much better. I'm sorry that you should have been subjected to such an unpleas –

– Please, ma'am. I pray you not to distress yourself on my account.

– Oh, *Norbert*! You make me feel ashamed for my own species.

– If I may be permitted to say so, ma'am, God's purposes are as mysterious as they are infinite.

– Indeed they are, Norbert. Can I offer you a drink?

– A glass of milk would be most welcome. I do not indulge in strong liquor.

– Well, I'm afraid I do, Norbert, and just now I feel I need one pretty badly.

– Of course, ma'am. Would you like me to –

– No, no. You sit there ...

– Your very good health, ma'am!

– To our success, Norbert! Ah, I needed that. Now let me see. Where had I got to?

- You had just reached Desmond, ma'am.
- Yes, of course, Desmond. Now Desmond we placed on a solar grid station in Libya. The report we had was that he had settled in very well, was liked by everybody and was extremely eager to please.
- Very like Alvin he sounds, ma'am.
- Oh, quite remarkably. Except of course that so far as we know there has been no more sign of eidetic regeneration in Desmond than there has in Bruce or Colin.
- Then what is it that makes you believe that Alvin is recovering ma'am?
- Don't mistake me, Norbert. It's only a very slender hope. But this vision of the girl does sound extremely promising. Now you *are* quite certain that Alvin said the angel was the one he'd seen at Aldbury?
- I recollect his words distinctly, ma'am. 'This is Cheryl,' he said. 'She's the one I saw yesterday. She's going to help us.'
- Excellent! Now, Norbert, I don't for one moment wish to suggest that your Cheryl was *not* an angel – indeed her behaviour seems to have been considerably more angelic than several of that species I might choose to name – but it is just possible that I might be able to get in touch with her through a certain Government organization known as the Samaritans.
- Why, ma'am, that's just what she called herself! 'I'm a Samaritan,' she said. Naturally I had no reason to assume other than that she spoke in good faith.
- Oh, I'm sure she did, Norbert. But we have nothing to lose by ascertaining whether my supposition is correct. Would you mind passing me volume 'S' of the directory? ... Thank you ... Now all that remains is for us to pray that they are prepared to co-operate.

18

Brother Dominic chewed his rosary thoughtfully and tried the Bristol Street number again. ''Tis not like Cheryl at all, at all,' he muttered. 'Come along, girlie. What's keepin' you?'

In apartment 50621 the videophone chirruped like a lovesick cricket, but no one came in answer to its plaintive call. The illuminated timeteller flipped on to 0032 hours. Water gurgled derisively in a wall pipe.

Brother Dominic thumbed the phase-in button and put on his official face. 'Ah well now,' he smiled, 'is it quite sure y'are that t'was Samaritan Cheryl ye were wantin'?'

'Quite sure,' said Professor Poynter's image firmly.

'Then I'm afraid I'm havin' t'disappoint ye. She's away off on a call.'

'Do you know when she'll be back?'

'Well now, I'm havin' t' confess t'ye that I don't. Isn't that the shameful admission for her boss t'have t'be makin'?'

'Then would you be so good as to give me her number?'

'Ah now that I can't do. T'be honest with ye I've been stretchin' the rules like elastic in admittin' t'ye that young Cheryl's in our Ministry at all, at all. T'would be more than me life's worth t'divulge classified information. I'm sure ye'll be understandin' that.'

Professor Poynter frowned. 'I can assure you that my business with Cheryl is in no sense connected with her official activities.'

'Sure an' don't they all say that?' chuckled Brother Dominic. 'Ah ye can have no idea o' the sort o' kinkies we get phonin' in. Why they seem t' expect us t' hand round the girls' numbers like a plate o' sandwiches! As if there wasn't far too much o' that sort o' carry on already! 'Tis enough t'make a saint fornicate!'

Professor Poynter assumed her most frigid official tone. 'Then am I to take it that you are in fact refusing to give me vital information – information which, I repeat this, may well be of inestimable importance not only to my Ministry but to the nation at large?'

Brother Dominic winced as though he had bitten on a bad tooth and his smile became distinctly queasy. 'Ah sure now, ye wouldn't be wantin' t'drive a man into a corner, would ye, Professor? Look, I'll tell ye what I'll do. As soon as young Cheryl gets back I'll be after givin' her yer message and yer number. Now a man can't do fairer than that can he? I mean then it's up t' her, is it not?'

'Very well,' said Professor Poynter. 'My number is 12-127-6692-3114. I shall be expecting a call within the next hour. I trust there is no further need for me to stress the urgency of the situation.'

'No, no, not at all,' Brother Dominic hastened to reassure her. 'I have the number down here. I'm givin' ye me word of honour as a Samaritan that I'll make it all as clear t'her as daylight. Now just you hang on there and before ye can say *Requiescat in pace* she'll be poppin' out of yer auld screen like a leapin' leprechaun.'

'Thank you,' said the Professor coldly, and leaning forward she pressed the erase button.

Brother Dominic's plump features were still a fading glimmer on the Professor's screen when a metal door was dragged open in the concrete warren under what had once been Pall Mall and young Alvin was helped over the threshold by an anthropoid boot up his tail. He stumbled forward, tripped over his own feet and, as the door clanged shut behind him, collapsed in a sprawling heap beside a pile of latex-foam mattresses which were stacked against the far wall of the dark cell. As he groped about his fingers touched something soft and warm. 'Holy hellebore!' sighed a familiar but weary voice. '*Not another!*'

At that instant a dim light was switched on from outside in the passage. Heaving himself on to his knees Alvin peered down at the dishevelled figure who was lying with closed eyes, half submerged in the drift of yielding foam.

'*Cheryl!*'

Like two pale mauve petals the amazing eyelids wavered doubtfully open and the jewelled eyes contemplated him warily. 'Oh, hello,' she said. 'It's you, Alvin. Where have you been?'

'Are you all right, Cheryl?'

A faint smile curled the corners of her lips. 'All what?' she murmured.

'What have they been doing to you?'

'I suppose *you*'d say they've been taking advantage of me,' she chuckled. 'I thought you were number eight.'

'Oh dear,' cried Alvin dismally. 'That's *terrible*!'

Cheryl sighed. 'It could have been a lot worse. After all, the bed's soft.'

'But *eight*!'

'Seven. It might have been five, actually. I think two of them went round twice. It was hard to tell.'

'But did they . . . ? Was it . . . ? Have you ever . . . ? *Before* . . . ?'

Cheryl chuckled. 'Well, only since I was nine. I was a slow starter.'

'Was that with apes too?' asked Alvin wonderingly.

Cheryl yawned. 'Well, not to start with of course.'

'But you *have* . . . ?'

'Oh sure I have. One or two. Just for kicks. You know how it is.'

'No, I don't,' said Alvin sadly. 'Doctor Pfizier said it was being impure. And Doctor Somervell said I ought to be thoroughly ashamed of myself.'

'That really is too bad,' said Cheryl sympathetically. 'Those two ghouls sound as if they ought to be locked up. Do you mean to say you've *never* done it?'

'I don't *think* so,' said Alvin cautiously. 'I'm not really sure.'

'Well, if we ever get out of this dump alive, I'll show you what all the fuss is about. I'd do it now if only I didn't feel quite so bushed.'

'Oh, thank you,' breathed Alvin. 'Norbert *was* right! You really *are* an angel!' and taking her hand in his he kissed it reverently.

Cheryl grinned. 'You're a nice boy, Alvin,' she said, 'even though you did get us into this mess. Daddy'll probably have a stroke when they put the squeeze on him for a hundred thousand. Specially seeing as it's the U.A.B. Still I daresay he'll see sense if they play it right.'

'They were going to let me go,' said Alvin. 'But I wouldn't without you.'

'You're not serious?'

Alvin nodded. 'Captain Comrade told me I was no use to them. He said you were an arch-enemy of the proletariape.'

Cheryl groaned disgustedly. 'That phoney jerk! I'd rather have fifty apes on top of me than have to listen to his sort of political crud! What's he hoping to achieve with his pathetic revolution? All he wants is to be at the top of the pile instead of the bottom. But it'll still be the same stinking pile!'

There were footsteps outside in the passage. The door opened and Maggie shuffled in carrying two plastic mugs of coffee. 'Cheered up, hev we?' she cackled. 'Well this'll put some lead in yer pencil.'

Cheryl sat up and accepted the mug she was handed. 'I hope you aren't dishing this out to the boys in the back room,' she grunted. 'I've had quite enough of them for one night.'

'Ah, she's a gel after me own heart,' chuckled the walnut-faced crone. 'But they won't be bothering you no more, me pet. Captain's blown his top. Seems what those monkeys got up to weren't no part er the official species struggle. 'N fact he's sent me along on purpose t'apologize.'

'There,' said Alvin, beaming round at Cheryl. 'Isn't that nice? I *knew* he had a kind heart.'

'Three cheers for the political ethic,' gurgled Cheryl. 'I'd have appreciated it more if the message had got through half an hour ago. Still, better late than never.'

'That's my gel!' cackled Maggie. 'Here, jer wanter drag?' She grubbed a stub end of a cigar out of her apron pocket and proffered it to Cheryl who rejected it with a shudder. Maggie shrugged, thrust the battered stogie behind her ear and shuffled out.

Alvin got up off his knees and sat down beside Cheryl on the mattresses. 'I wonder what's happened to Norbert,' he sighed. 'I miss him like anything.'

Cheryl's private opinion was that Norbert was probably floating face-downwards in the Serpentine by this time but she did not want to depress Alvin further by suggesting it. 'I daresay Dominic'll be having kittens too,' she said. 'I was supposed to be on call between midnight and two.'

'What *do* you do, Cheryl? Really?'

'I'm a Samaritan.'

87

'Well. I know that.'

'So?'

'So what do Samaritans *do*?'

'You really don't know *anything*, do you Alvin?'

'You don't *really* kill people, do you?'

'We don't *kill* people,' said Cheryl. 'Our job is to help people who want to kill *themselves*. It's work of national importance.'

Alvin pondered this in silence for a while. 'Why is it?' he asked at last.

'Well, because there are too many people,' said Cheryl in the tones of one who explains a fact so patently obvious that it seems unbelievable it should need explaining at all.

'But why are there too many?' pursued Alvin.

'Because people go on having babies, of course.'

'But *why* do they, Cheryl?'

Cheryl shrugged.

'I thought women were only *allowed* to have two.'

'Only *supposed* to have two,' she corrected. 'There's no *law* against them having a dozen. They tried that one back in the nineteen-nineties and look where it got them.'

'Where *did* it get them?'

'Well, the Compulsory Abortion Riots and all that stuff. All those governments collapsing one after the other. *You* know. *History*.'

'Oh,' said Alvin.

'Then when the apes were invented it got even worse. I mean they had to *have* the apes to do all the jobs that no one else was prepared to do, but the apes had to be fed and so on or they couldn't work. So really it was just like having a whole lot more people. Well, in a way they *are* people, aren't they?'

Alvin nodded.

'The government tried all sorts of things,' mused Cheryl. 'Special baby taxes and withholding allowances and so on, but none of it seemed to make much difference, because at the other end the doctors were all madly trying to keep people alive to about a hundred and fifty. And it was the old ones who made the decisions. They weren't going to give anyone the right to kill anyone else, because they were all afraid they'd be the next ones to get the chop. Why, do you realize, Alvin, it was only fifty years ago that they actually got round to repealing the *suicide* laws! Since then they've tried all kinds of ways of getting people to do themselves in. I think that business in the Park must've been one of them. You see it's quite all right *legally* as long as people are prepared to do it *themselves*.'

'But, Cheryl, why *don't* people just have fewer babies?'

'I don't know,' she said. 'Instinct, I suppose. Dominic says they'll never solve the problem till they discover something nicer and cheaper and more readily available. And no one's come up with *that* yet! Anyway lots of people just say it's God's will.'

'Maybe it is.'

Cheryl shrugged. 'Some God!'

'Don't you believe in Him?'

'Do you?'

'I'm not sure,' said Alvin. 'Norbert says God is Love.'

'Protein for Norbert. And I daresay our dear Captain would say God is Power. It makes about as much sense. More maybe.'

Alvin swirled his coffee slowly round in the bottom of his mug. He thought of those sad heaps of corpses lying under the trees. It had happened but it still didn't make any sense. How happy they had all been shouting and singing together. Slow tears of grief and perplexity began to fill his eyes. Where the sandbag had landed his head seemed to be throbbing worse than ever and he had an eerie sense of something vast and threatening brooding up behind him like a huge thunderhead. Tiny shivers skittered up and down his spine. The skin of his arms and legs began to gather itself up as though intent on shrinking him out of existence. He was becoming nothing and everything. The shivering became more and more violent until his teeth were chattering like a typewriter. The mug slipped from his inert fingers and clattered to the floor.

'Are you feeling all right?'

He felt Cheryl's hand alight on his arm and he tried to nod in affirmation while all the time one part of him was crying '*Hang on!*' and the other begging '*Let go!*'

'I,' he gasped 'I–I–I . . .' and then it happened. A blinding white soundless explosion behind his eyeballs and a wild rushing gale that battered his eardrums and then, as swiftly as it had come, faded away to a whisper in the remote distance, leaving his aching head a-swirl with a crazy kaleidoscope of jumbled images.

He blinked his eyes. Between his feet the trail of spilled coffee gleamed like an ebony snake. On his forearm lay Cheryl's fingertips pink as anemones. His lost identity streamed back into his consciousness like sand in a twisted hour-glass. 'Alvin Forster,' he whispered. 'I am Alvin Forster, an eidetic freak. *And there are four of me.*'

19

I T WAS NO part of Pinkerton's job to assess the security value of the information he dug up, but he had been working for MOSS long enough to recognize the difference between gold and pyrites. As he slouched back in the monitor-station loafer and overheard Professor Poynter describing to Norbert how Alvin and his brothers had come into existence he knew beyond a shadow of doubt that he had at last made the strike which every security agent dreamt about. Corruption in high places was the MOSS equivalent of a 24 carat virgin seam. In an access of sudden panic he re-checked that the recorder was functioning correctly, then, having satisfied himself that it was, he cleared his first ever 'Red A' priority channel to headquarters and began piping this precious bane straight through to K.G.3.

– Ever since that day, Norbert, I have been tortured with self-doubt. What was it in me that compelled me to destroy this miracle at the very moment it had been vouchsafed to me? Can *you* tell me that?

– I daresay ma'am that a miracle could well be a very unnerving experience. When one is alarmed one does not always act in the most sensible way.

– Then you are prepared to take my word that it *did* happen?

– Certainly I am.

– But *why*, Norbert?

– Well, ma'am, in my experience things are only rarely what they seem to be. Do not forget that I knew young Alvin well. I perceived in him the fountain head of something wholly pure, some force for good that he himself was unaware of. Alvin moved through a world that lay all about him but was visible to him alone. In his presence I could not but feel a better ape and realize that the Kingdom of God was at hand.

– Ah, Norbert, if only I had been blessed with a little of your simple faith when my hand seized upon that cannister of A-12, the world might be a different and a better place today.

– Who can say, ma'am? Is God's path ever a straight line? Perhaps if I'd brought Alvin to you yesterday, you'd still have looked on him as an experiment.

– Yes, that's true. It took the nightmare to make me realize what I had created. That, and you too, my dear friend.

– God has chosen us both, ma'am, just as he has chosen Alvin.

– But to what end, Norbert?

– Ah, there, ma'am, I must confess you have the advantage of me.

– Let me tell you what I think. You are the first person in the world I have dared to say this to, but I have come to believe that there is a latent power residing in those four clones which may yet transform the world. What this power is I cannot guess, but it is up to us to see that it does not fall into the wrong hands. I tremble to think what MOSS or *Minisoc* might do with it! We have no time to lose, Norbert! Alvin *must* be found!

– And then ma'am?

– You and I will re-unite the four of them, Norbert!

– Very well, ma'am.

– Why it's 01:55 already! Surely Cheryl should have returned by now? I can't believe that she is still out on that same call. I shall contact that unpleasant man again.

Meanwhile in the intestinal labyrinth of K.G.3 the magnetized silicate threads were busily spooling up a cocoon of guilt to hatch the larva of Miriam Poynter's destiny. By 0200 hours she had already confessed enough crimes to have consigned any ordinary citizen to the abattoirs twenty times over. But the licence which her high office allowed her meant that each sentence she uttered had to be semasiologically analysed and then checked against a special M.O.P. security index. This process was so laborious and so potentially corruptive that the work had to be parcelled out among a regiment of technicians, none of whom was permitted to examine any sequence of more than three phrases. Consequently a full K.G.3 analysis sometimes took so long to complete that by the time guilt had been incontrovertibly established the incriminating material had already been de-classified. No less a person than Sir Gordon Loveridge had, all unknown to himself, twice come within a whisker of indictment only to glide away to safety on the toboggan of an international scientific congress from which his classified indiscretions were trumpeted to the world and hence automatically de-classified. Indeed it had been remarked with some justification that the mills of MOSS ground so fine that the particles they eventually produced were often invisible to the human eye.

In Professor Poynter's case what had been immediately apparent to Pinkerton was by no means so obvious to the subtle scrutineers of K.G.3. Better than any they knew that, in the realms of science, nothing was ever quite what it seemed to be. 'These cases are never simple,' they murmured. 'This time there must be no mistake. A false accusation of High Treason could ruin us all. We must watch and wait.'

20

CHERYL'S FEARS THAT her father might react unfavourably to a demand for ransom from the U.A.B. were certainly justified. He was summoned from the forum of his exclusive West End Dream Club where he was taking a central role in *The Rape of the Sabine Women*, given a perfunctory squirt from a de-hallucinant atomizer, and informed that there was an urgent call for him on the videophone in the Senior Members' zoned sanctum. Without bothering to remove his centurion's helmet, Sir Harold Langridge M.P. (for he was, in truth, no less) strode, sword in hand, up the carpeted gangway and, rattling and wrathful, demanded to know what the hell it was all about.

'I really couldn't s-say sir,' panted the be-wigged flunky who had brought him the message. 'Lady Langridge only s-stressed that it *was* extremely urgent.'

'The mean bitch!' fumed Sir Harold. 'She knew I'd drawn Centurion for the first time in six months! You could at least have stalled her off for another five minutes.'

'I tried to, sir. Indeed I did. B-but you know her Ladyship.'

Sir Harold grunted, thrust open the door of the sanctum and marched up to the screen. 'Well, Miranda?' he barked. 'What is it? And you'd better make it good!'

The woman who stared at him out of the screen looked like a slightly older model of her own enchanting daughter. 'Bad news, I'm afraid, Harry,' she said 'Cherry's been kidnapped.'

'*Kidnapped!*'

She nodded. 'We've just had a demand for a hundred thousand pounds from the U.A.B.'

'The devil we have!' roared Sir Harold, wrenching savagely at his plaited leather chinstrap. 'No bloody monkey's getting a hundred thousand out of me! Tell the bastards they can keep her! And good luck to 'em!'

'They say if we don't pay up they'll send us her ears by special delivery tomorrow lunchtime.'

Sir Harold snorted. 'Ears! Dammit, Miri, she can get herself a brand new pair for a thousand each! It's blackmail, that's all it is! Blackmail!'

'Yes, dear. I know.'

'Why didn't you get on to Reggie at Security? Hell, we pay far too much bloody tax as it is!'

'I've already spoken to him, dear. He advises us to pay up.'

'The devil he does! It's not his hundred thou!'

'He says there's really not much hope of our seeing Cherry alive again if we don't.'

'The stupid little tramp!' howled the outraged father. 'How the hell did they get hold of her anyway?'

'It was in the Park, I believe.'

'*The Park!* Was she stoned out of her tiny mind! By God, Miri, I'll get every cent of this back out of her wages if I have to squeeze her from now to Doomsday!'

'Then you *will* pay?'

'Why the hell should I? Aren't Samaritans insured against occupational risks?'

'I'm not sure if this comes under "Line of Duty", dear. Do you want me to find out?'

'You bet I do! And Miri –'

'Yes, dear.'

'You tell the U.A.B. from me that I'll have their guts for garters if it's the last thing I do!'

'Yes, dear. Oh, there is one other thing.'

'Well?'

'They're insisting on maximum publicity.'

'The devil they are! We'll see about that.'

'I gather they've already been in touch with the I.V.S.'

Sir Harold saw his wife glance down at the floor. 'Go on,' he growled menacingly.

'They're suggesting we could auction off the So-Vi rights to the negotiations for the hand-over and split the proceeds fifty-fifty.'

A gleam of pure acquisitive admiration kindled in Sir Harold's eye. 'By God, Miri, you've got to hand it to those chimps for nerve!'

Lady Langridge glanced up again. 'They seem to think we could hold out for at least two hundred thousand.'

Sir Harold's eyeballs flickered round like computer spools. 'Phew!' he whistled. 'Two hundred thou, eh? Cool, Miri! Bloody cool!'

Lady Langridge coughed. 'They actually suggested that this was Cherry's own idea.'

For the first time Sir Harold's face broke into a slow, wide grin. 'Of *course*!' he cried. 'That's *it*! No bloody monkey could be *that* sharp! I always said my little girl was wasting herself in Samaritans! Why in five years she could own half the bloody City!'

Lady Langridge permitted herself the ghost of a smile. 'They said that you would be allowed a free hand to do the financial negotiating.'

'That's my poppet all right!' crowned Sir Harold. 'She knows her daddy! By God, she does! How'm I supposed to contact these junglies?'

'They'll be phoning through again in an hour. Do you want it relayed?'

Sir Harold unclipped his helmet and dragged it off. 'I'll come home,' he said. 'I'm off the boil now anyway. Be with you in twenty minutes, Miri. You get hold of Willy Probe right away and tell him to alert the C.B.S. and the E.B.C. I want a four-cornered, security-sealed link-up with them and the I.V.S. *Two* hundred? By God, Mrs Langridge, I'm beginning to think that if we play our cards right we'll more than double that!'

21

CHERYL WAS WOKEN from a profound sleep by the sound of the cell door being opened. One of the young uniformed apes who had earlier regarded her as 'perks' in the species struggle was standing in the doorway. 'You're to come with me, Miss,' he said. 'Captain's orders.'

'Oh go and eat bananas,' growled Cheryl. 'And that goes for him too!'

'Your father wants to speak to you on the videophone, Miss.'

'So what?'

Alvin who was lying on another mattress in the corner of the cell woke up and demanded to know what was going on.

'I've had a summons from Captain Marvel,' Cheryl informed him. 'It seems my ever-loving pappy's on the line.'

'Oh,' said Alvin. 'That's nice.'

Cheryl did not seem convinced. 'Except that I've already made it plain to our pocket Trotsky that I'm not going to do his dirty work for him. Go on, you,' she growled at the ape. 'Clear off, and let me get some sleep!'

The chimp unshouldered his laser and pointed it at her rather unsteadily.

'And don't try any more of the strong-arm stuff, buster,' she said icily. 'If you lay another finger on me your stupid hide won't be fit for dish rags and you know it.'

The laser wavered indecisively and then swivelled round till it was pointing at Alvin. 'So *he* gets it,' said the ape.

There was a long tense moment while Cheryl debated whether her aura of immunity could be extended to include Alvin and decided it couldn't. 'All right,' she muttered, 'I'll come. But don't think you've had the last word, lover-boy.'

She swung her legs off the bed and slid them into her boots.

'Shall I come with you, Cheryl?' said Alvin.

'You stay, pinkie,' grunted the ape.

Cheryl pressed the static seals on the backs of her calves and stood up. 'You're sure you won't feel safer if I was blindfolded?' she enquired sweetly.

'Captain didn't say anything about that,' muttered the ape. 'Come on.'

The cell door clanged shut behind them and the sound of their echoing footsteps died away in the distance. Alvin stood up and tested the door but it was bolted fast. Then he lay down on Cheryl's bed, switched on an eidetic mental street guide to London and tried to work out where they were. Presumably somewhere within walking distance of Marble Arch. He rummaged around in his incredible memory until he had found an old print map which marked underground car parks. The only suitable one seemed to be Green Park. He then went back and began combing retrospectively among the vaults and passages he had been led through, bringing them up one by one before his mind's eye and scrutinizing them minutely for some possible clue. Within a minute he had found what he was looking for – a faded red arrow on a concrete span girder and a scarcely legible inscription, EXIT HALF MOON ST. A quick flick back to the street guide and he had pinpointed to within a hundred yards his exact location. It was as though the last jig-saw fragment of his identity had slotted neatly into place. He knew *who* he was; he knew *where* he was. All that now remained was to discover *what* he was!

He thatched his hands behind his head and gazed up at the rust-stained concrete of the cell-roof. Having selected an area about three feet by four he simply recreated within it the video-screen on which, three years before, he had watched Professor Poynter's stereoscopic image telling him that he was unique. He followed it through from beginning to end and pondered upon it. Had she been telling the truth? Presumably only up to a point, which was certainly one of the reasons they'd wanted to get their own back on her. 'They'? *He!* That was what the old duck hadn't realized. It wasn't just a case of 4 times 1, but of 1 to the power of 4! Or maybe even 4 to the power of 4! One is one and all alone and ever more shall be so, but turn your mirrors inwards on themselves and who can count the images then?

So what *had* happened? He closed his eyes and opened them again upon Desmond and Colin and Bruce, who were but Alvin and Alvin and Alvin. Four to the power of four. But four *what*? 'Clones' she had called them. 'I am we,' he murmured, 'we are I.' Could it be that Professor Poynter was their *mother*? Had they banished her because she had betrayed them? Well, of course they'd given her a fright, but surely she'd asked for it. Present a kid with a pair of seven league boots and what do you expect him to do? *Polish* them? But maybe she *had* done the right thing after all. The right thing for the wrong reasons. Psychological re-structuring and three years in limbo had made a lot of difference. And if *he* was different, so were they all. There wasn't much likelihood of them making the same mistake again. But if only she'd waited a moment before she'd squirted that can of gas at them. It would only have needed a moment. Just long enough to tell her . . . or maybe to *show* her . . . yes, to show her . . . And, lying there in the gloom remembering it, Alvin's lips curled into the same sublime grin that had once graced the clones' moony features as they lay unconscious on the floor in the Ministry of Procreation.

That was how Cheryl found him when she returned, escorted by a different guard, half an hour later. She walked over to the bed and looked down at him. 'Alvin Forster,' she said, 'I hate to tell you this, but that's my bed you're sleeping on.'

Alvin's eyes blinked open. 'Oh hello,' he said. 'What happened?'

Cheryl sat down and began pulling off her boots. 'I've been too clever by half,' she grunted. 'It looks as though we may be stuck here for at least a week.'

'A week! But I thought . . .'

'So did I,' said Cheryl. 'But I overlooked one thing. Daddy's infallible nose for business.'

'He won't pay?'

'Oh, he'll *pay* all right, but now he's insisting on 60 per cent of the world So-Vi rights.'

'*So-Vi rights?*'

Cheryl gnawed her lip. 'I suppose I should have told you this before, Alvin. I put the idea up to the Captain at our first interview. I thought they'd be able to make a sort of sob feature out of it. You know the kind of thing. "*M.P.'s lovely young Samaritan daughter held hostage by urban guerrilla apes.*" It seemed a good way of recouping the ransom.'

'Hey, Cheryl, you know that's really clever!'

'Um,' grunted Cheryl, 'what I forgot was that it takes time to build these things up. The So-Vi boys reckon on a week for maximum impact. Believe it or not, darling Daddykins was ready to give 'em a fortnight! He says it'll take him that long to get really haggard.'

'And did the Captain agree?'

'*Him!*' Cheryl snorted bitterly. 'He just can't wait to get his paws on all that lovely loot. Hell, he's even been offering to make me the U.A.B. fund raiser! So much for the holy species struggle, eh? God, Alvin, this world makes me puke, really it does.'

'What're you going to do?'

'I don't know,' she sighed. 'I'll think of something. Right now I just want to catch up on my beauty sleep.'

Alvin took the hint, sat up and relinquished the bed. 'Hey, what happened to that guard?' he said. 'The one who was going to lase me?'

'Oh, him,' yawned Cheryl. 'I fixed him all right. I swore to the Captain that he'd tried to rape me again. He's had his laser confiscated and been given a week in the cookhouse. That'll teach him to tangle with his superiors.'

22

SHORTLY BEFORE 0800 hours the next morning Professor Poynter was roused by Norbert informing her that a man describing himself as a P.I.D. sergeant was at the door and wished to speak to her.

'What does he want?' she whispered, sitting up in bed and reaching for her wrap.

'He wouldn't say, ma'am. Shall I let him in?'

'Show him into the study, Norbert. I'll be with you in a moment.'

She leant over and kissed Hortense who was still deep in a drug-induced oblivion, then she slipped out of bed and tip-toed from the room closing the door softly behind her.

As she entered the study the visitor turned to her, introduced himself as Sergeant Atwell from the Political Investigation Department of Urban Security, and asked if she was Professor Poynter.

She nodded. 'You wished to see *me*, Sergeant?'

'Yes, madam. I'm at present engaged on the Langridge investigation under Chief Superintendent Tugwell.'

'The *what* investigation?'

'Langridge, madam. Miss Cheryl Langridge, the only daughter of Sir Harold and Lady Langridge, was kidnapped by terrorist apes at approximately 2200 hours yesterday evening and –'

'You did say *Cheryl* Langridge, Sergeant?'

'Yes, madam. She's being held to ransom for £100,000. Now we have been informed that at approximately 0030 hours this morning you videophoned the Samaritans and asked very particularly to speak to Miss Langridge. You phoned again about an hour later. Would you mind telling me why?'

Professor Poynter blinked. 'I – er – wished to ask her some-thing.'

'Yes, madam,' said Atwell patiently, 'we rather imagined you did. Now would you be so good as to tell me what that something was?'

Professor Poynter was silent for five long seconds. 'I hoped she might be able to help me locate a person I am particularly interested in.'

'And who is that?'

'His name is Alvin – Alvin Forster actually – but at present he is answering only to Alvin.'

'I see,' said the Sergeant. 'Can you describe him to me?'

'I can show you his stereograph if you'd prefer it.'

'I certainly would,' said Atwell.

Professor Poynter fetched her album from the desk, opened it and pointed to Desmond. 'That was taken three years ago,' she said, 'but it's still a very close likeness.'

'May I?' said Atwell, and producing a miniature camera he rapidly snapped three quickies of the clone. 'This lad, he was a friend of Miss Langridge's?'

'Not that I know of.'

'A client, perhaps?'

'I hardly think that likely.'

'Then why should you have hoped to contact him through her?'

'Because I have good reason to believe that Alvin was last seen in her company.'

'Oh yes?' said the Sergeant. 'What reason?'

The Professor hesitated momentarily. 'Norbert, the anthropoid who let you in just now, was Alvin's closest companion. He reported the fact to me.'

Atwell's eyebrows twitched. 'You mean he was *there*? With them?'

Professor Poynter nodded.

'Where was this?'

'In Hyde Park.'

'Well, well,' said Atwell enigmatically.

'I can assure you that Norbert is absolutely blameless in this matter, Sergeant.'

'In that case you won't object to my questioning him, then?'

'Of course not. Shall I call him?'

'I'd be obliged, madam.'

The first thing Atwell's trained eye noticed when Norbert entered was the eavesdropper adhering to his belt. 'Excuse me,' he said and, reaching out, picked it off and examined it. Then, without speaking, he circled slowly round the mystified chimp and peeled off the second bug. Pressing them so that they clung together he turned to the open window and flipped them out. 'Someone's obviously interested in you,' he said. 'Any idea who?'

'No, sir,' said the astonished Norbert.

'You know what those were?'

Norbert shook his head.

'Body static micro-transmitters.'

Norbert and Professor Poynter eyed each other in dismay.

'What were you doing in Hyde Park yesterday evening, Norbert?' asked Atwell.

'He was trying to –'

'Please, madam, let him answer for himself.'

'We were in this protest march, sir,' said Norbert.

'Oh yes?' said Atwell. 'Who were you with?'

'The Crewys Road Anti-Vasectomy League. But all we were doing was trying to get to the Suburban Expressway.'

'You're sure it wasn't the U.A.B. crowd?'

'No, sir,' said Norbert. 'I don't think there was one.'

'But if there had been you'd have been with it, eh?'

'Sir,' said Norbert with impressive dignity. 'I am a branch leader of the Anthropoid Scientific and Technical Workers' Union. We do not recognize the U.A.B.'

Atwell sniffed sardonically. 'All right,' he said. 'Go on from there.'

Norbert described his adventures of the previous night with such unaffected sincerity that even the cynical Sergeant was finally convinced that he was telling the truth. 'I'm beginning to wonder if they haven't maybe got your young friend as well,' he muttered. 'But if that's the case why haven't they put the squeeze on for him too?'

'On whom?' enquired Professor Poynter. 'Alvin is of absolutely no political significance.'

Atwell looked at her and decided not to say what he was thinking.

'I'm most anxious to get him back,' she said. 'Do you think that if I could get in touch with these guerrillas myself they might be prepared to release him?'

'We aren't even sure that they've got him, are we, madam?'

'But if he was with Miss Langridge . . .'

'We don't even know *that* for sure, do we?'

'How *would* one set about getting in touch with them?'

'If you'll take my advice, ma'am, you won't try it. Believe me, I know how these U.A.B. jokers tick.'

Norbert turned and looked gravely at the Professor. 'I will find him for you, ma'am.'

'Oh, Norbert! *How*?'

'God will lead me to him.'

Atwell coughed. 'Well, I'd best be getting along. You've both been most helpful. We'll get in touch with you the minute we hear something definite. In the meantime my advice would be to sit tight, cross your fingers and pray.'

'Thank you, Sergeant.'

Professor Poynter saw him to the door. As he was going out he turned to her and murmured: 'It's none of my business, I know, madam, but I'll take a bet with anyone that those bugs I found on your friend were MOSS standard hi-fi. Good day to you.'

As soon as she had closed the door behind him Professor Poynter hurried through into her bedroom and began a metiulous examination of her clothes. Since she now knew what to look for it did not take her long to locate the two eavesdroppers Pinkerton had planted. With her heart racing she peeled them off and dropped them down the kitchen disposal. Then summoning Norbert to assist her she inched her way round the apartment searching for others. The fact that they found none did nothing to dispel her profound sense of foreboding. 'It must mean they've heard every word we said last night,' she said.

'Then they will know about Alvin, ma'am.'

'And not only about Alvin.'

'What are we going to do?'

'Find him before they do, Norbert. It's our only hope.'

23

THE CHERYL LANGRIDGE story erupted on Europe's breakfast screens that morning and followed the sun around the globe. By lunchtime her exquisitely wistful stereoscopic features had unloosed enough tears to float a medium-sized rocket carrier, while on the other side, close on forty thousand apes had flocked to join the illicit ranks of the U.A.B.

From Fremantle to Finisterre a billion mums drooled and snivelled as the cameras panned pathetically round the little empty apartment in Bristol Street, lingering on the empty A-G. harness; on the knapsack of variegated venoms; on the Adonis Mk V paramour (a seventeenth-birthday present from her dear old granny); before fading out on the inevitable close-up of Cheryl's graduation stereo-still of herself in full flight, administering the kiss of death to a plummeting stock-broker over Hounslow.

By 2200 hours it had become plain to the professionals that they had stumbled once again on the age-old winning formula – the truly human sob story. Cheryl's young life was opened up like a can of seafood and the processed tit-bits forked out on to the plates of the starving multitude. They gobbled them up, sucked their fingers and howled for more. Sir Harold and Lady Langridge were hounded from house to House and put on an award-winning performance of tight-lipped Anglo-Saxon nobility – the tightness of Sir Harold's lip certainly accentuated by the fact that he had been forced into accepting a last minute compromise of 55% instead of the 60% he had hoped for.

Cheryl's neighbours were interviewed singly and in groups and, after drawing their word-pictures for an enthralled audience, drew their appearance cheques for themselves. Brother Dominic pronounced his solemn curse on the U.A.B. and his equally solemn benediction over his missing acolyte before using the rest of his slot to plug the selfless dedication of the Samaritans.

Then, as the So-Vi sleuths buzzed back and forth like blue-bottles over the golden carrion of Cheryl's last hours before the snatch, the vital element of mystery without which the story would never have earned its niche in the temple of the truly greats, miraculously appeared – 'Mr. X'! Yes, her transvestite neighbour *had* heard voices from Cheryl's apartment that evening ('these walls are as thin as paper you know, dear'); no, she/he hadn't heard what they were saying ('What *do* you take me for, love?'); but, yes, it *could* have been a man's voice – well, a boy's, anyway.

Tally ho! and the hunt for the villain/lover/go-between was up. The camera hounds sniffed their way down the Bristol Street arcade and accosted the natives. 'Yes, Cheryl *had* been with a boy. A fair-haired chap. No, they hadn't noticed him particularly. *Ordinary* seemed to describe him best. Gone towards the Park they had. Well, into the Lane, anyway. Oh, a *lovely* girl, Cheryl! Such a shame! Her poor mum and dad!'

A Security Guard with his back to the camera (no faces: no reprisals). 'Yeah, he remembered her. Wearin' a sort of hood thing she was. And the bloke wiv er? Moon-faced sort of a git, wiv stickin' aht ears. He'd told 'em t' 'op it quick afore they got copped.'

An I.V.S. exclusive with Chief Superintendent Reginald Tugwell of Urban Security and (wholly co-incidental therefore unmentioned) the husband of a major shareholder in the So-Vi company conducting the interview. 'Yes, undoubtedly these kidnap cases were very, very tricky. One false move and you could have Miss Langridge's pretty head in a plastic bag. He could assure the public that every possible step was being taken and a number of positive leads were being followed up. No, he wasn't prepared to say what they were at this stage. What was his personal opinion of the U.A.B.? He would rather not say. Was he not on record as having referred to them as "misguided idealists"? No comment.'

Sir Harold Langridge M.P. (cornered in the conveniently photogenic portico of Chuffles' Club): 'These blackguards must be brought to book. Until that happens none of us could sleep safe in our beds. Was he going to pay up? He was being advised by Chief Inspector Tugwell. Had the U.A.B. contacted him personally? No comment. Was it true he had gone into the "No" lobby against the "Votes for Apes" motion last June? He had never made any secret of his opinion on these matters. Did he consider his daughter had been singled out because of his extreme views? Young man, I do not consider my views extreme. Well, good luck, Sir Harold. Thank you. Good day.'

So finally back to Brother Dominic again for a background fill-in. 'Well, now, that's quite true, she was out on a call earlier yesterday evenin'. No, they hadn't recorded the call. Why hadn't they? Well, it wasn't Samaritan practice, that's why. Well, yes, he supposed it might have thrown some light on what had happened to her, but there, he was hardly in a position to say, was he?'

24

SOME HOURS LATER the Captain walked into the room where Cheryl and Alvin were sitting playing chess. It was far better furnished than the first cell they had occupied. He contemplated the game in silence for a moment then said to Cheryl: 'I've just had 'em on the phone again.'

'Lucky old you,' she muttered.

'They say the bloodstained messages aren't emotive enough.'

'You're really breaking my heart.'

The Captain sucked his teeth noisily. 'They're asking for something tangible. An ear, maybe?'

'Well, they're not getting one of mine,' said Cheryl firmly. 'Let them find their own if they want one.'

The Captain examined the dead end of his cigarette and nodded towards Alvin. 'One of his wouldn't do, I suppose?'

'Definitely not,' said Cheryl. 'Don't be ridiculous.'

The ape contemplated Alvin's remarkable aural appendages which promptly turned a delicate rose pink under the scrutiny.

'They don't look *real*, do they?' he said at last. 'Well, how about a finger then?'

'Look,' said Cheryl, 'I'm telling you straight. It's not on. They can get a whole fistful of fingers if they want them. Arms, legs, the lot. You aren't trying to tell me it's beyond the wit of those So-Vi phonies to fix a simple thing like that. Either they make do on our heartbreaking messages and find their own bits and pieces or the whole deal's off. Got it?'

The Captain sniffed. 'You capitalists are all alike,' he grumbled. 'When it comes to a question of principle, it's always self first. Selfish, that's what you are. What could sacrificing a bit of yourself for a noble cause mean to someone like you?'

'Not much if you must know,' said Cheryl. 'And if it's a cause as phoney as the U.A.B., nothing at all. All you're interested in is power.'

'All politicians are interested in power,' replied the Captain blandly. 'That's why they're politicians.'

Cheryl snorted. 'And what do you suppose you'll do if you ever get it?'

'*When* we get it,' he corrected. 'It's simply a question of time. The dictatorship of the proletariape is an inevitable historical process.'

'And what we're doing here now is a part of that, I suppose?'

'Of course. Wasn't it your Chairman Mao who taught us that to reach the top of a mountain you travel by a winding road? U.A.B. membership has already increased by over two hundred thousand, thanks to you. You're our biggest recruiting boost since we rubbed out the Lord Chief Justice in '68!'

'And I thought it was a good idea,' muttered Cheryl disgustedly.

The Captain shrugged. 'Another week of this and I reckon we'll be strong enough to come out into the open. That means you'll have helped the species struggle to skip a whole generation. Enfranchisement's the next step. Come the election after next I'll be leading the U.A.B. into Parliament. It wouldn't surprise me to end up holding the balance of power in Brussels.' He relit his cigarette, jutted his lower lip and blew a jet of smoke over the table. 'That offer I made to you is still open, by the way.'

Cheryl burst out laughing.

'I mean it. You mark my words. As the man said: Nothing succeeds like excess. The moment we reach the million mark we'll have the liberal pinkies falling over themselves to identify with our cause. It's only a question of time.'

Alvin, who had been listening in fascination to this exchange, decided the time had come for him to put in a word. 'But you still haven't told us what you'll do when you *do* get power, Captain.'

'As a matter of fact I'm in the middle of drafting a new party manifesto,' said the Captain. 'The old one's a bit too rough and ready seeing as how we're broadening our base. I've turned up some useful material from one of your 20th-century pinkie demagogues. How d'you like this? *I have nothing to offer but blood, toil, tears and sweat!* Got just the right sacrificial ring, don't you think?'

'But isn't that just what you've always said the apes have got already?' objected Alvin.

'When will you grow up, simp?' groaned the Captain. 'Of *course* it's what they've got already. Apes are born to suffer – it's the only thing they know how to do. What I'm offering them is the sense of *purpose* to go with it.'

'And what *is* the purpose?' enquired Alvin deferentially.

'Freedom, of course.'

'But freedom from *what*?'

'Oppression,' said the Captain. 'Tyranny and oppression.'

There was a sound of running feet in the passage outside. An anthropoid aide burst into the room and saluted perfunctorily. 'We've scooped a pinkie and an Albert, Captain,' he panted. 'Found 'em wandering around in the Green Park tunnels.' He jerked his head in the direction of Alvin. 'They say they've come to find *him*.'

'Armed, are they?'

'No, Captain.'

'All right, I'll come.' The Captain took a pace towards the door then changed his mind. 'No. Bring 'em along here.'

The aide saluted again and ran out.

'I wonder how they got through the So-Vi screen?' mused the Captain. 'All the exits are supposed to be covered. You can't trust anyone these days.' He walked over to the wash-basin in the corner of the room and peered at himself in the speckled mirror.

'D'you know who they are?'

'I suppose it *could* be Norbert,' said Alvin.

'That the A.S.T.W. chimp you told me about?'

Alvin nodded.

The Captain smoothed back the hair over his ears. 'And the pinkie?'

'I've no idea.'

Footsteps tramped down the passage; halted outside the door. 'Come in!' growled the Captain.

'Inside, you!' barked a chimp guard.

The door opened.

'*Norbert!*'

'*Alvin!*'

'Stay where you are!' yelped the escort.

Norbert and Professor Poynter, looking travel-stained and rather knocked about, shuffled to a halt in the centre of the room and blinked around them. Norbert had a pronounced swelling over his left eye and the Professor was bleeding from a gashed lip.

Alvin, who had risen from his seat as they entered, now ran forward and embraced Norbert tenderly.

'That I should have lived to see it!' growled the astounded Captain. 'How the hell did you two get in here?'

'From the basement of Lancaster House,' said the Professor dabbing at her lip. 'Sergeant Atwell told us there was a way through from there.'

'And who the hell's Sergeant Atwell?'

'A Political Investigation officer.'

'So that bunch are in on the act, are they? I might have guessed. And what are you then?'

'I'm Professor Poynter of the M.O.P.'

The Captain was visibly taken aback. 'And you're sticking your neck out for *him*? What's going on around here?'

Professor Poynter turned to Alvin and regarded him much as the father of the Prodigal Son might once have regarded his contrite off-spring. 'I could not rest until I'd found him,' she said. 'You won't remember me, Alvin, but I –'

'Oh, but I do, Professor. It was you who laid me out at the M.O.P.'

'*You remember that!*'

Alvin grinned and nodded.

'But this is *marvellous*!' she exulted. 'Absolutely marvellous! When did it happen?'

'The day before yesterday,' said Alvin.

'What the hell *is* all this?' demanded the Captain turning upon Cheryl. 'Do *you* know?'

She shrugged. 'He got his memory back. We think it might have been something to do with his being gassed and then knocked out.'

'So?' said the Captain suspiciously. 'What's marvellous about that?'

'You'd better ask her,' said Cheryl. 'She's the authority on the subject.'

'Spill it, Prof.'

Professor Poynter suddenly realized that by giving vent to her enthusiasm she might have lessened the chances of freeing Alvin from captivity. 'I was responsible for his tragic accident,' she said. 'I feel as though a tremendous burden of guilt has been lifted from me.'

'Oh, is *that* all?' said the Captain morosely. 'Myself I preferred him as he was. Not that you'll notice much difference. He's still an idiot.'

'He is a child of God,' said Norbert indignantly. 'Blessed are the pure in heart.'

The Captain pulled a disgusted face. 'Don't come that religious crap with me, monkey! I was fed texts as protein substitute for ten stinking years.'

Norbert screwed up his eyes and squinted across at his captor. 'Don't I know you?' he enquired slowly.

'Could be,' admitted the Captain. 'St Barnabas Mission mean anything to you?'

Recognition dawned on Norbert's face. 'Young Piker!' he exclaimed. 'Lead alto. Excommunicated for bootlegging sacramental wine!'

The Captain grinned. 'That's right. Then who're you?'

Norbert chuckled. 'Have you forgotten Magnify-the-Works-of-the-Lord-and-Exalt-His-Name-for-Evermore Jones?'

'*Evermore Jones!* Well, I'll be flogged! Then where's this "Norbert" handle come from?'

Norbert shrugged. 'I lost my faith back in '53 and spent a couple of years wandering in the wilderness. I swopped names with a chimp who took a fancy to mine.'

'Well, well,' chuckled the Captain. 'It's a small world, Evermore. And how did you come to fetch up at – what's the name of the place ? – Aldbury ?'

'That chimp I told you about was down for a Government rehabilitation course. I went along in his place and opted for Hydrological Agronomy. That's all there is to it really. And how about you, Piker ?'

'I lived on my wits for years till I got framed for a hi-jack job and bought a twelve-month stretch in '56. Did some reading inside. Got to hear about the U.A.B. Haven't looked back since.' The Captain took off his glasses and massaged the bridge of his nose. 'Why don't you join us, Evermore ? Plenty of scope in the movement for an honest monkey like you.'

Norbert shook his head. 'Don't think I don't appreciate the offer, Piker, but I've heard my own call. Loud and clear, this time. That's why I'm here.'

'Not *him* ?' said the Captain nodding at Alvin.

'That's right.'

'But what's so special about this simp ? Apart from the fact that he's the only pinkie I've ever known who's greeted an ape like a long-lost brother.'

'Maybe that's it,' said Norbert.

'Ah, you're still the same old dreamer, Evermore. Remember that Easter sermon you preached on "Blessed are the meek for they shall inherit the earth" ? Best sermon I ever heard. We could certainly use you in Propaganda.'

'It's nice of you to say so, Piker, but it strikes me you're doing pretty well on your own account. You always did have an eye for the main chance.'

'Oh we're really going places this time! You've heard how they're falling over themselves to join the U.A.B. ?'

Norbert nodded. 'Each to his own, Piker.'

The Captain shrugged. 'I suppose you know what you're doing but I'm flogged if I do. Still, you're welcome to him if that's what you want. And good riddance, I say.'

'Thank you,' said Norbert and Professor Poynter in unison.

Alvin looked at Cheryl and shook his head. 'I can't,' he said. 'Not without Cheryl.'

The Captain sat down on one of the beds, took out his tobacco pouch and prepared to roll himself a cigarette. 'I told you he was an idiot,' he said. 'You won't find another like him.'

'I love her,' said Alvin. 'I'll go when she goes.'

'You'll go when I say so,' growled the Captain.

'And *I'll* go when *I* say so,' chipped in Cheryl. 'Anyway you don't need me any more.'

'Have you gone crazy too?' spluttered the Captain. 'You aren't due for release till nine on Saturday evening! That's the way we planned it! You're getting peak slotting on global channels!'

'Oh that's all right,' said Cheryl. 'I was going to ask them to fix me a stand-in anyway. I couldn't have carried it off myself. Not without laughing.'

'You didn't tell me that,' protested the aggrieved Captain.

'I only thought of it just now,' admitted Cheryl.

'Do you think it'll work?' asked Alvin.

'Bound to. They're sure to prefer it anyway. It'll give them time to rehearse.'

Professor Poynter gasped. 'Do you mean to say you've *planned* all this?'

'Oh well,' shrugged Cheryl, 'not altogether, of course. It just seemed too good a chance to miss.'

'I *see*,' murmured the Professor. 'So *that's* why Sergeant Atwell turned so co-operative. How many people are in the secret?'

'I've no idea,' said Cheryl, 'but there's bound to have been some leaking along the line by now.' She pushed back her chair and stood up. 'I suppose I'd better go and get things sorted out with Daddy,' she said. 'Are you coming, Captain?'

The Captain opened his mouth as if to object and then shrugged helplessly. 'And I thought I'd seen it all,' he muttered. 'Compared to her a corkscrew's straighter than a bloody laser.'

'Oh don't be such a pathetic cube,' said the world's favourite heroine.

25

THE BREAKING OF the eavesdropper contact on Professor Poynter had flung MOSS into a state of remarkable perturbation. This was largely accounted for by the fact that their last scrap of recorded conversation had suggested that their old rivals the P.I.D. were muscling in on the territory. An urgent command to Pinkerton, to re-establish the broken link forthwith, might possibly have succeeded had he not been fast asleep when the message came through. By the time he was fully alerted and had been despatched at the double to Kew Mansions, the Professor and Norbert had already left.

Having reached the door of the Professor's apartment and failed to get any response to his ringing, Pinkerton let himself in with a MOSS codebreaker key and set about bugging the apartment against the Professor's return. In the course of this operation he entered the darkened bedroom where, unknown to him, Hortense was still lying asleep. He was planting an eavesdropper on the back of the dressing-table mirror when she woke up and, still half-hallucinated, took him for the Professor and drowsily invited him back to bed.

It was not the first time in his professional life that Pinkerton had been in roughly similar circumstances. He groped round for the satchel in which, along with the other tools of his trade, he carried an amnesiac aerosol for use in just such an emergency. Unfortunately he had left the satchel in the other room and he was about to tiptoe off in search of it when his feet became entangled in the pile of de-bugged clothes which the Professor had left scattered on the floor. He staggered, lurched wildly around, arms windmilling, and pitched forward across the semi-recumbent form on the bed.

For Hortense he was the embodiment of all the traumas of her youth. Her arms and legs contracted in an hysterical spasm of what was either terror or lust or a mixture of both, and the horrified security agent found himself locked to the naked bosom of a vigorous and comely lesbian. 'Please let go, madam,' he begged in a strained whisper, terrifyingly conscious of the micro-transmitters in his pocket all busily relaying this back to K.G.3. 'You'll ruin my career.'

Hortense's reply was to grip him the tighter and mutter: 'Get it, you black brute! Get what you've come for!'

'Madam, it's all a mistake,' whimpered the anguished Pinkerton. 'I'm an anthropoid.'

'You're a black bastard,' moaned Hortense. 'A great black randy gorilla and you're raping me.'

'No! No! I'm not!' squeaked Pinkerton, struggling frantically to free himself. 'How can you say such things? Oh, please let me go, madam.'

Hortense's lissom thighs held him gripped like a pair of nut-crackers. Her strength was as the strength of ten while Pinkerton, paralysed with fear, felt as though all his tendons had been severed. He made one further feeble effort to wriggle free and then abandoned himself to despair. His last desperate act was to close her mouth with his own in a futile attempt to prevent her from incriminating him beyond all hope of reprieve. This merely had the effect of goading her into a further paroxysm of carnality which culminated in her grabbing the eroticon spray from the bedside table and drenching them both in an impenetrable concupiscent miasma.

The MOSS semasiological analysis of the sound patterns trans-mitted from the Professor's apartment during the next twenty minutes took four days to complete and ruined over half a million pounds' worth of ultra-sophisticated electronic hardware. By the time it was concluded Pinkerton had resigned from the Service and was enjoying a life of luxurious depravity as the simian paramour of Hortense Poynter (nee Çalabash), a post which, incidentally, he filled with energy and imagination until he succumbed to over-stimulation and perished in the late Autumn of 2073.

Although Norbert and the Professor were unaware of these developments they benefited from them to the extent that it was several days before the MOSS bloodhounds were unleashed to cast about for their cold scent. Long before then the fugitives, together with Alvin and Cheryl, were speeding in a hovercraft up the eastern seaboard of Scotland bound for the rocky islet of Aukinsay in the Orkneys where, ignorant of his history, the second of the clones passed his days as 'Brother Bruce' a novitiate monk in the monastery of Saint Clumbert.

Cheryl's presence in the party was explained partly by her father's having insisted as the condition of her release that she must remain out of sight and incognito until the ransom negotiations and their inevitable aftermath were over and forgotten, but partly also by her own thirst for adventure and her growing attachment to young Alvin. As she admitted wryly to herself on more than one occasion, there *was* something about the boy . . .

Once the arrangements for Cheryl's So-Vi 'double' had been concluded their release from the confines of the U.A.B. headquarters had followed rapidly. Captain Piker had insisted to the last that he would always find places for Cheryl and Norbert in his organization and they had parted on the best of terms. Now, disguised as tourists, the four friends were seated in the passenger lounge of the *Sir Compton Mackenzie* sipping at a selection of beverages and watching the So-Vi recording of Cheryl's return to the land of the living. Several of the other passengers were already weeping unashamedly as the cameras cut back and forth between the deserted rendezvous near the Albert Memorial, the tense and noble faces (expertly tensed and ennobled by courtesy of the E.B.C. make-up department) of Sir Harold and Lady Langridge, and the familiar – but oh how infinitely pathetic! – little empty bed in Apartment 50621 Bristol Street.

Just when the tension seemed to have been racked to breaking point there was a pale, will-o'-the-wisp flicker among the shadowy elms in the direction of the Round Pond, a well-rehearsed gasp from the commentator and, as the cameras zoomed in, behold! Cheryl herself tripping barefoot over the dewy grass clad in what looked rather like a ragged Victorian nightie.

Spontaneous applause and a chorus of 'ooh's and 'ah's broke out in the lounge of the *Sir Compton Mackenzie*, and one maudlin matron was even moved to cry out: 'Och, the puir wee bairn.' Whereupon Cheryl, overcome with sacrilegious mirth, choked on her gin and bitters.

The substitute Cheryl was an Italian drama student named Marina Fabriota who spoke only broken English, but this did not matter at all since her dialogue had already been pre-recorded by a voice-double. As far as looks went the likeness was wholly remarkable, and the retinal blanching and dyeing which had transformed a pair of dark brown eyes into emerald green ones gave even Alvin momentary pause to wonder which was the real Cheryl and which the imitation.

They heard her recount her adventures while tears of the purest glycerine trickled down her pallid cheeks. Yes, she had been treated with commendable courtesy. No, she had no idea where she had been held. Who was the mysterious Mr X? Samaritans never disclosed the names of their clients. Then he *was* a client, not a member of the U.A.B.? Certainly he was not a member of the U.A.B. How had she spent her time in captivity? Writing poetry and worrying about Mummy and Daddy and little Pookie her pet goldfish. What did she want most? A really hot bath and a long, long sleep. And so on and so forth. She even managed to get in the mild plug for the U.A.B. which Captain Piker had insisted upon.

By the time it was over, Cheryl and her companions scarcely knew whether they were suffering from nausea or excessive admiration. 'I don't know what fee she's being paid,' shuddered Cheryl, 'but she's earned every cent of it. *Little Pookie!* Ugh! I couldn't have managed that if my life had depended on it!'

'But what will you do when you get back?' asked the Professor. 'You'll have to play up to the role, won't you?'

'I *couldn't*,' Cheryl insisted. 'That chapter's closed for good.'

'Then won't that mean your giving up the Samaritans?'

'It looks like it, doesn't it?' she nodded. 'I think I'd probably have had to anyway. They're pretty sticky about us preserving anonymity.'

'Then what *will* you do?' asked Alvin.

'I haven't really thought about it,' she confessed. 'My rake-off will give me enough to get by on for a couple of years. After that – who knows? Maybe I'll take up the Captain's offer. I'll think of something.'

Alvin regarded her with unadulterated worship. 'I think you're *fantastic*, Cheryl! Really I do.'

'I think I'm pretty fantastic too,' grinned Cheryl. 'It's just something I'll have to learn to live with.'

26

SAINT CLUMBERT'S ABBEY was not in itself an old foundation though it occupied the site of one. It had been re-established in 1987 as one of the simulated environment retreats for the world-weary, and it now provided a 21st-century blend of convenience and pseudo-austerity admirably gauged to the needs of its clients. Indeed, many of them had experienced something very close to a genuine mystical revelation as they had lain quaking in their air-conditioned cells listening to the equinoctial gales raving among the granite turrets and praying that the roof would not be blown away. After such experiences they usually returned to the urban treadmill spiritually refreshed and re-conciled to their lot.

Abbot Fox, the present leader of the community, was a man of principle who took his duties seriously. To his way of thinking 'simulated environment' meant something very different from the Disney/Butlin type of plastic-and-plaster fake-up that could be found up and down the country offering 'a randy, roistering week-end in Nell Gwyn's Cheapside' or 'two days' glorious mill-bashing with the Luddites (sledgehammers and crowbars provided)'. At Saint Clumbert's it was hessian habits and rope-soled sandals for all, and heaven help any skrimshanker who was found slipping an extra battery into his electrically-heated underwear. What with compulsory attendance at matins, nones, vespers and the rest, even the casual visitor left Aukinsay with some inkling of what monastic life might have been like in the Dark Ages. The odd thing was that many of the pilgrims returned again, year after year, and one or two had even left their bones in the abbey graveyard.

Not that it was all prayer and fasting. Each week there was a feast day in honour of some doubtful saint or other and the visitors were always encouraged to share in the various menial activities that occupied the permanent staff. Besides the kitchens and the garden there was a goat flock and two fishing boats that required constant attention. Nets and lobster pots were always in need of repairs, and, for the more creative individuals, a line in driftwood sculpture had recently been introduced and was proving a considerable attraction. All in all it was a busy and flourishing little community which surely justified the modest £250,000 per annum Government subsidy which kept it going.

A raucous swirl of seabirds greeted the *Sir Compton Mackenzie* as she hove to some three hundred yards off shore and lay wallowing in the windy swell while a longboat, pulled to the stirring rhythm of a lustily bellowed psalm, shot out from the little jetty at the foot of the beetling cliff. As it bobbed alongside, half a dozen rather dazed-looking repatriates were helped aboard the hovercraft and then Professor Poynter, Alvin, Norbert and Cheryl scrambled down to take their places. With a loud hosanna the tonsured coxwain gave the order to back oars. 'Pull for the Lord, my lads!' and they were away, rising and swooshing over a foam-streaked sea the colour of dirty dishwater, back to the sanctuary of the jetty.

As they scrambled ashore they were welcomed by Brother Fred who blessed them perfunctorily before conducting them up a short flight of granite steps into a shallow, artificial cave which contained an antiquated though perfectly serviceable elevator. This then began winding them up rather grudgingly to the Abbey at the top of the cliff.

'In the days of the first foundation they used to have to flog up three hundred and sixty-five steps,' Brother Fred informed them. 'One for each day of the year. Some of our visitors still like to do it but we don't encourage it since we lost a couple from suspected vertigo the summer before last. Still, the Lord doth provide. They made good bait for the lobster pots. How long are you here for?'

'Only a short stay,' said Professor Poynter. 'We've really come to see Brother Bruce.'

'Oh, him,' said the monk and then tipped back his cowl and peered at Alvin. 'You wouldn't be his twin brother by any chance?'

'Yes,' said Alvin.

'I thought as much. Bit surprised though. I mean to say any-one round here would lay you a penance to a couple of illuminated brevaries that our Brucie was a one and only. Manifold are the works of the Lord, eh?'

'What does he do here?' asked Alvin.

'Goat herd,' said Brother Fred. 'We tried him on the fishing but he kept falling in the oggin and we had to spend half our time lugging him out and giving him the kiss of life. Same thing in the kitchens. Hadn't been at it a week before he slices off the end of his thumb with a cleaver. Willing lad, mind you. Nothing's too much trouble for him. He's safe enough with the goats. They like him and he likes them. Seem to understand one another, you might say.'

'He sounds just right for Saint Clumbert's,' said Cheryl.

'Well, yes and no,' agreed the monk. 'I mean, let's face it, this isn't what you'd call a *real* monastery. Not *really* real, if you take me. But Brucie now, he's just about the one hundred per cent genuine article. Why only last week I heard the Abbot say, "If we don't watch out our Brother Bruce will be walking on the water one of these days." He meant it too. Still, since you know him I daresay you'll take my drift.'

'Another dweller in the Realms of the Spirit,' murmured Norbert.

'You might say that,' allowed Brother Fred. 'Lost his memory or something, hasn't he? Not that it's any of my business. He's in a bit of a dream most of the time. Sees visions and what not.'

'What sort of visions?' enquired the Professor sharply.

'Oh, we don't take much notice of them. The other day he was on about some angel or other. Couldn't stop talking about it. Happy as a sandboy he was. Singing his head off while he milked his goats. Oh, he's a great one for the visions is our Brucie.'

The lift shuddered to a halt. Brother Fred clattered open the safety gate and ushered them out. 'We'll get you booked in straight away,' he said, 'then I'll wheel you down to the habitary and see you're kitted up. If you'll just follow me . . . And if you won't mind my saying so, the lowered eye always gives a nice impression to the staff.'

An hour later, robed and sandalled, they were ushered into the presence of Abbot Fox. Norbert, who insisted on wearing his cowl, was having some difficulty in preventing it from slipping down over his eyes but, this apart, they made a suitably reverential quartet.

They discovered the Abbot kneeling in prayer before a small illuminated shrine. He did not look up as they entered. They waited in silence till he had concluded his devotions. Finally he crossed himself, climbed to his feet and turned to face them. 'Welcome, in God's name, to Saint Clumbert's,' he said, and then his eye alighted upon Alvin. He frowned. 'Brother Bruce, you are neglecting your duties.'

'Oh, I'm not Bruce, M'Lord Abbot. I'm his brother.'

'You presume to jest with me, Brother?'

'It's quite true, Abbot,' said Professor Poynter. 'This is Alvin, Bruce's twin.'

'And who might you be, madam?'

Professor Poynter explained and introduced the others, including Cheryl who, for some obscure reason, had chosen the temporary alias 'Blossom Chatsworth'.

The Abbot nodded. 'Yes, of course, I remember, Professor. Sir Gordon Loveridge mentioned your name to me when he sent me Bruce. I was not aware that the lad had a twin. He has never spoken of him.' He returned his attention to Alvin. 'The likeness is certainly extraordinary. I could not have told you apart. Does your brother know that you are here?'

'I don't think so, M'Lord.'

'You are aware of his present employment?'

'He's goat-herd, isn't he?' said Alvin.

'And an extremely good one, I'm pleased to say. The milk yield has increased by some 20 per cent since your brother was given charge of the herd. He has established a truly remarkable *rapport* with his flock.' He turned to Cheryl and treated her to a long, shrewd stare. 'Your face also seems strangely familiar, Miss Chatsworth,' he said. 'I can't imagine why.'

Cheryl who had already noted the large So-Vi screen in a corner of the study, smiled and shook her head.

The Abbot shrugged. 'Well, as you will already have realized, here at Saint Clumbert's we prefer not to do things by halves. Our patron saint should perhaps have been Konstantin Stanislavsky. He, you may recall, preached that "illusion" and "reality" are but two sides of the same coin. To the dreamer his dream *is* real. Or, to put it another way, reality is essentially subjective. Hence our insistence upon the offices and trappings of our Order.

'The monastic diet is simple but adequate and wherever possible we eschew the ersatz in favour of the genuine. Our cheese, incidentally, is something of a gourmet's speciality. I recommend you to try it with a black bread. The cells, which at first glance may strike you as somewhat sparsely equipped, contain all the essentials, and you will find the pallets surprisingly comfortable.

'Sexual activity is discouraged but not forbidden. For those who feel the urge very strongly we have instituted a number of pre-lapsarian indulgences of varying severity. A list of these is posted in each cell. They range from one day's compulsory fast for masturbation to a public flogging of both parties for those wishing to copulate.' The Abbot treated them to a wintry smile as he added: 'You may or may not be relieved to hear that these strictures are relaxed between 20.00 hours and 24.00 hours on our feast days. During those four hours the facilities of our well-appointed stimulatory are available for such as care to make use of them.'

Cheryl grinned. 'And when's the next feast-day, Abbot? Just out of curiosity you understand.'

Abbot Fox twitched an ascetic nostril. 'Today, as it happens, Miss Chatsworth. This is the anniversary of The Venerable Cusp – an early Ionian mystic of somewhat dubious authenticity who gains a brief mention in the Lindisfarne Chap-book. I shall be preaching a short sermon on him at supper this evening.'

'I look forward to hearing that,' said Cheryl. 'He should go down well with the cheese.'

Abbot Fox gave her a thoughtful stare but forebore to comment.

'Would it be possible for us to visit Bruce now?' enquired Professor Poynter.

'If you can find him, certainly,' replied the Abbot. 'He will probably be out on the hills somewhere. Failing that the lad will undoubtedly be present at this evening's feast. They are the one repast he never seems to forget.'

Professor Poynter expressed the thanks of them all and then they bowed and shuffled out of the austere presence.

'I shouldn't wonder if M'Lord Abbot handles the floggings

himself,' murmured Cheryl. 'Wasn't that a cat-o'-nine-tails he had over the fireplace?'

'A flagellum, certainly,' agreed Professor Poynter, with a trace of something akin to wistfulness in her voice. 'I must say I hadn't realized that Saint Clumbert's would offer such interesting attractions.'

27

THEY DID NOT succeed in running Brother Bruce to earth, nor was he present at the evening service in the chapel, though doubtless many of those who were, and who saw Alvin there, would have been prepared to swear on oath that he was Bruce. The last benediction having been given the congregation trooped out across the wind-swept courtyard and into the refectory where the long oak tables were waiting to receive them. A fire, fed with huge baulks of dried driftwood, crackled and sputtered and flicked out tongues of bright blue flame. Real candles flamed in the wrought-iron sconces and mouth-watering cooking scents wuffed in from the adjacent kitchens.

Visitors and staff having taken their places behind the benches, a brief grace was spoken by the Abbot from the elevated lectern. He then lowered his hands as a signal for everyone to be seated, bowed his head for a moment in silent prayer and then, when the shuffling had subsided, raised his eyes and looked up and down the long hall. There were some seconds of absolute silence when even the fire refrained from crackling. The Abbot lifted his bony hands and gripped the edges of the lectern. 'Dearly beloved brethren,' he said and his quiet, precise voice, relayed by a series of concealed speakers, could be heard clearly in every corner of the great hall. 'This evening we meet to pay homage to the shade of the Venerable Cusp, a man of whom little is known, and who, indeed, perhaps never existed at all except in the fertile imagination of the anonymous scribe who penned that extraordinary document we have come to know as the Lindisfarne Chap-book.

'The facts (if we may call them that) which he retails about Cusp are certainly somewhat bizarre, for he informs us that this venerable soul was hatched from the egg of a puffin, raised in solitude upon a sea-girt rock, converted the seals by virtue of his golden tongue and still more golden example, and was carried by them to the shores of Hoy in order that he might prevail upon the heathen, who, at that time, were occupying these isles.

'The heathen for their part were reluctant to change their allegiance and remonstrated with the missionary, their remonstrance taking the somewhat extreme form of hacking him into four quarters with a broadsword. However, they had reckoned without the spiritual tenacity of their adversary who promptly reconstituted himself and continued to preach to them as though nothing had happened. The butchery was thereupon repeated, but so was the miraculous reformation, until, in the end, realizing the force of Christian argument, they desisted and were baptized upon the shore.

'We are told little more of the Venerable Cusp other than that he lived to the ripe old age of one hundred and seventy-three years and that in the course of the Lenten fasts he was frequently observed to float in the air. During the high winds of the vernal equinox it was sometimes necessary to anchor him to the ground by means of large stones placed upon the hem of his habit.'

The Abbot paused and seemed to fix each one of them with his cold grey eye. 'Personally,' he continued, 'while remaining somewhat sceptical as to the strictly factual accuracy of our anonymous hagiographer, I do believe, most sincerely, that the Venerable Cusp *ought* to have existed, for he was manifestly the possessor of great faith, goodness and simplicity. In short, a truly holy man. Therefore I feel that we have a duty to his creator, as much as to the saint himself, to meditate in silence for a few minutes upon the holiness of the Venerable Cusp, to whose hallowed name I hereby dedicate this evening's solemn feast.' So saying, Abbot Fox bowed his head and proceeded to do just that.

Scarcely more than half a minute had passed in contemplative silence when a small lych door, which was standing ajar in the furthermost dark corner of the refectory, squeaked painfully open and Alvin's brother crept deferentially into the hall. An expression of the most intense wonder illuminated his placid features and he slowly raised his hands in an attitude of profound, even yearning supplication. As he did so the flickering candlelight seemed to dim and to flow away down the hall towards him, where, from a shimmering refulgence, it congealed precipitately into a single radiant image *of a stark naked Cheryl Langridge*!

There was a smothered gasp from those mundane souls who, regrettably deficient in spiritual discipline, had interrupted their meditation to take covert note of Brother Bruce's entry. The ripple of their astonishment travelled down the hall, gathering substance as others raised their eyes and beheld the incredible cause of the disturbance. When it reached Cheryl herself she too glanced round, beheld her naked self floating suspended some four feet in the air, and let out a loud, startled yelp.

Her cry dropped like a stone into a pool. The image shattered into a thousand fragments, dissolved, and was gone. Only the wonderstruck clone was left, his hands still lifted in stunned adoration, seemingly oblivious of the sensation he had caused.

Hearing Cheryl's outraged exclamation, Alvin, the Professor and Norbert had all glanced up – as indeed had Abbot Fox – just in time to catch a glimpse of the vision that had evoked it. Now the four friends regarded each other and slowly shook their heads in unison. 'I'll swear that was Bruce,' whispered Alvin, 'I could feel him doing it.'

'Are you sure you weren't helping him?' growled Cheryl.

Alvin blushed scarlet and lowered his eyes while the murmurs of wonder swelled into a buzz which grew steadily in volume until the Abbot tapped the lectern microphone with his fingernail and restored the hall to silence. 'Brother Bruce,' he enquired coldly. 'Was that manifestation your doing?'

'M-M-M'Lord Abbot?' mumbled the petrified clone.

'I repeat my question, Brother. Was that – that –' the Abbot groped for the word he wanted '– that *succuba* your creation?'

Brother Bruce blinked tearfully and scrubbed his scalp with his knuckles. 'I – I don't know. M'Lord Abbot.'

'You don't *know*?' repeated the Abbot incredulously.

'I –I haven't seen her without her clothes on before, M'Lord.'

At this a few depraved souls risked a snigger and were immediately frozen into silence by the Abbot's icy glare. 'And just what do *you* think she was, Brother Bruce?' he enquired silkily.

'A holy spirit, M'Lord?' was the clone's timorous suggestion.

'A holy spirit,' echoed the Abbot flatly. 'Miss Chatsworth, would you be so good as to stand up for a moment?'

Cheryl frowned, glanced round at the others, then rose hesitantly to her feet. At once a renewed murmur of astonishment broke out among those who had witnessed Brother Bruce's vision.

'A holy spirit, Brother Bruce?' repeated the Abbot. 'A *holy* spirit? Really?'

The clone's face resembled a palimpsest in which mortification was scribbled over incredulity. 'M'Lord,' he groaned. 'Oh, M'Lord.'

His unaffected anguish pierced young Cheryl to the heart. She smiled and stretched out her hand to him in welcome. 'So I'm to be your angel too, am I?' she said. 'Well, why not?'

The Abbot who had been secretly relishing the opportunity for a little further humiliation of the simple monk now found, unaccountably, that the appetite had left him. A faint smile fitted across his thin lips. He shrugged. 'Let the feast begin!'

As the kitchen doors crashed open and a dozen tonsured chimps marched into the hall bearing huge steaming dishes, Cheryl left her place and moved to where Brother Bruce, completely overcome with emotion, had subsided on to his knees in an attitude of prayer. She reached out her hand and catching hold of one of his ears coaxed him gently to his feet. 'Come on,' she said, 'we've been keeping a place for you.'

'She speaks! She moves! She *is*!' murmured the enraptured clone. '*Jubilate Deo!*'

Cheryl released his ear and transferred her grip to his arm. 'What did you *do* just now?' she whispered, leading him up the hall to where the others were waiting. 'Do you know?'

'I prayed to the Venerable Cusp,' said Bruce.

'For *me*?'

Bruce nodded.

'Holy hemlock!' gurgled Cheryl. 'You don't suppose *he* was the one who undressed me?'

Bruce looked as though his face was on fire. 'Yes,' he whispered. 'The dirty old man!'

'Oh *no*!' cried the clone. 'He only wished me to worship you unadorned, radiant in beauty as the rising sun!'

'Well, I must say he could hardly have chosen a more public place for it,' said Cheryl.

'He meant only to be kind,' said Bruce. 'I know he did.'

Cheryl grinned. 'Maybe it's just as well it's a feast day, Brother, or we could both have been in trouble.' She released his arm and gestured towards the others. 'Well, here we are. Do you know anyone?'

During their passage down the hall Bruce had had eyes only for Cheryl herself. Now he looked round. The first face he saw was Alvin's. For a second he seemed simply stunned. Then his mouth dropped open and an expression of genuine agony twisted his features. He staggered up against the table, clasped his hands to his head and gave vent to a frightening high whinney of pain.

As he did so, Alvin too was overcome by a sudden excruciating migraine which seemed to drive up into his brain like a white hot iron spike. Just when it seemed that his skull must inevitably split and fall apart, the agony ceased as suddenly as it had begun. At the identical moment Bruce too lowered his hands, blinked, and looked about him. 'Alvin?' he murmured. 'It *is* Alvin, isn't it?'

Alvin nodded. 'It's been a long time, hasn't it?'

The two clones stared at each other with an intensity so totally exclusive that the others could almost feel their identities being leached out of them. They knew something extraordinary was going on but had no idea what it could be. Professor Poynter shivered involuntarily and found herself recalling the moment when she had told Sir Gordon that she knew how Rutherford must have felt. But it was too late now for second thoughts.

A servitor came up with a fragrant bowl of *bouillabaisse* which he proffered to them. Professor Poynter helped herself with a trembling ladle. While she was doing so, Bruce assisted Cheryl into her place and took his own opposite her. It seemed to Cheryl that all five of them had suddenly become marooned upon some mysterious island of stillness. Calmness descended upon her like twilight. She smiled at the ape who was handling her the bowl and helped herself. The questions she had been about to ask no longer seemed important; they too belonged to another world. She vaguely remembered something that Alvin had told her when they were in the cell under Green Park, something she hadn't understood then, but even as she tried to recall it it slipped away like the tissue of a dream lost in the waking. She raised her head and found the two clones were both gazing at her. Those April sky eyes, once so simple and so innocent, now seemed to her infinitely mysterious. Without knowing why she suddenly felt unhappy and, curiously, ashamed.

28

'ALVIN BEING ONCE more in control of his full eidetic powers was presumably in a position to restore Bruce's also. However, the fact that Bruce's individual vision was shared by everyone who had eyes and chose to look at it, does not necessarily mean that it had genuine three-dimensional existence. After all, it could have been a mass-induced hallucination.'

Miriam Poynter, her cheeks flushed with the mead she had drunk, leant forward and wagged her index finger at the two clones. They for their part gazed back at her owlishly.

Cheryl, the Professor, Alvin and Bruce were seated in a small pornarium off the stimulatory. From time to time sounds like the twittering of many little birds floated through from the adjacent room. These emanated from the oriental sound-track of *Golden Lotus* which was being projected in stereoscopic panavision to honour the anniversary of the Venerable Cusp.

The absent Norbert had wandered off quarter of an hour before in search of a toilet. Somewhat befuddled by unaccustomed alcohol he had missed his way back and was now sitting cross-legged on the upholstered floor of the stimulatory trying to make out what was happening both on the screen and in the roseate gloom around him. Long before he had succeeded in finding out, his cowl slipped down over his eyes and he surrendered himself to sleep.

'Well, of course it was an hallucination,' said Cheryl. 'What else could it have been? I mean to say it couldn't have been *me*, could it?'

Alvin and Bruce exchanged an enigmatic glance.

'Well, could it?' persisted Cheryl.

'No, of course not, my dear.'

'Then how do you explain that birth-mark?'

'Birth-mark?'

Cheryl nodded. 'I'm the only person here who knows about it. It's just here.' She pointed to a fold in her voluminous habit somewhere in the region of the left side of her chest. 'Go on,' she challenged. 'How do you explain that?'

The Professor frowned. 'But I'm sure you must have been the only one to notice it.'

'Oh yes?' said Cheryl, jutting her chin accusingly at the clones. 'Was I?'

They both blushed and lowered their eyes.

'Look here, Professor,' said Cheryl, 'isn't it time you told me just what you *do* know about them? It strikes me I've at least as much right to know what they are as you have. And what about *them*?'

Professor Poynter sighed. 'They know already, my dear.'

'Well, tell *me* then.'

The Professor frowned down at the floor, then, after glancing round to make sure she was not being overheard, began to recount the history of Alvin and his brothers.

Cheryl's emerald eyes grew wider and wider. 'Hey!' she whispered. 'They're *illegal*!'

'I'm fully aware of *that*,' said the Professor bitterly. 'I may say it's the very least of my present worries.' She went on to describe a few of the extraordinary events that had led to the clones being parted and concluded with her discovery that by this time, presumably, MOSS was aware of what she had done.

When she had ended Cheryl looked at her with a totally new admiration. 'Holy hemlock!' she murmured. 'You really have got yourself in a jam, haven't you?'

Alvin gave a deprecatory cough. 'Professor Poynter, Bruce and I are convinced that we must make direct contact with either Colin or Desmond – and preferably both – as soon as possible. As far as we have been able to ascertain, our power of manipulation is at present limited to the creation of three-dimensional visual projections. Although this may prove useful to us, it is only the first step towards the realization of our full potential. Functioning normally each one of us is capable of individual eidetic projection. Two of us working in concert are apparently able to give sufficient substance to our united vision for it to be shared by others. But this still leaves us in the realms of simple addition. However, when three of us are combined we believe we shall move into the sphere of multiplication.'

'And with four?' enquired the Professor tremulously.

'We are not yet sure ourselves,' said Alvin, 'but we suspect that four is something else again.'

'Such as what?' demanded Cheryl.

'Possibly the access to a hitherto unsuspected dimension,' suggested Alvin vaguely.

'And what's *that* in heaven's name?'

'We honestly don't know,' said Alvin, 'but we suspect we've stumbled on the key to an asomatic space/time continuum.'

Cheryl stared at them. 'You beat me up,' she said, 'you really do, Alvin. When I first met you in the Park I thought you were just some simple sort of goon who'd had enough of life. Now here you are using words I haven't even *heard of* to describe things I can't even begin to *think* about! I'm beginning to wonder if I wouldn't have done a whole lot better to have left you in the slaughterhouse.'

The two clones shook their heads in unison. They looked remarkably like Tweedledum and Tweedledee. 'But don't you see?' said Bruce. 'You're a part of it too. A part of *us*. That's why we both saw you. You *couldn't* have kept out.'

'Huh?' grunted Cheryl. 'Who says I couldn't?'

Bruce and Alvin looked at each other. 'I do,' they said with one voice.

'Does that make sense to you?' asked Cheryl turning to Professor Poynter. 'Because it certainly doesn't to me.'

The Professor sighed. 'Ever since I saw what *Minisoc* were

doing in the Park I've given up expecting things to make sense.'

'But that was different,' said Cheryl. 'What these two are saying is that us being here now *had* to happen because they wanted it to!'

'Only *you*,' said Bruce. 'She's an extra.'

'But I couldn't have got here on my own.'

The clones shrugged.

'And so what happens now?' she demanded. 'We all gallop off to find the rest of you, I suppose?'

Alvin and Bruce looked quite extraordinarily sheepish. 'Well, we thought . . .' they murmured, 'that first . . . perhaps . . .'

'Well, go on.'

'You *did* promise,' muttered Alvin.

'What did I promise?'

'To show us . . . me, I mean . . . what all the fuss was about.'

'What on earth are you talking about?'

'*You* know,' wriggled Alvin. 'Taking advantage . . .'

Cheryl laughed. 'Oh, *that*! I thought you'd forgotten all about it.'

'We've been thinking it might have been why we both saw you,' explained Alvin. 'We're not sure, of course.'

'And I'm not sure that I feel like it right now. Tomorrow maybe.'

'But it'll be a whole week till the next feast day,' pleaded Bruce.

'Isn't that a shame.'

The clones regarded one another quizzically while they appeared to ponder on this rejection. Finally Alvin said: 'Is it just that you don't feel in the mood?'

'You might say that.'

'And how would you feel if you were?'

'That,' said Cheryl, 'is not something you can explain in cold blood.'

Alvin frowned and then his face broke into a slow and rather crafty grin. At that instant, without realizing what was happening to her, Cheryl found herself back in her own little apartment in Bristol Street. A few minutes earlier she had landed with Alvin on her balcony and now he was standing before her while she quizzed him about Norbert. She knew only too well what he was feeling about her and her own knowledge filled her with a delicious sense of power and anticipation, together with certain other familiar inward ticklings and pricklings each in their own way as delightful as they were unmistakable. The retrospective experience lasted until Alvin insisted he must go and look for Norbert, whereupon, somewhat reluctantly, she relinquished him. As she did so she clearly heard him say 'Damn!' Immediately the familiar apartment was gone and she was again sitting in the pornarium gazing in bewilderment at the two clones, one of whom was saying crossly to the other: 'It's no use. We can't control it yet.'

'Hey, what's been going on?' she demanded.

'How do you feel?' they enquired apprehensively.

To be honest Cheryl was not at all sure *how* she felt, but she suspected that a yo-yo might feel much the same way. 'Did *you* do that?' she accused them.

'It didn't work properly,' said Alvin apologetically, 'but you see it was all we had to operate on. We thought that maybe now there were two of us we'd be able to bend things a bit. We really didn't mean to upset you. We just thought it might help.'

'Did you hypnotize me?'

'Well, I think it might be more accurate to say we individually hallucinated you.'

'But I didn't *want* to be hallucinated.'

'Oh, didn't you?' said Bruce, blinking at her. 'We thought you were rather enjoying it.'

It was Cheryl's turn to blush. 'That's neither here nor there,' she said firmly. 'The point is you had no right to do it without asking my permission first.'

'Well, we didn't know if we could do it at all,' Alvin pointed out. 'It was just an experiment.'

'Is that supposed to make it better?'

'I don't know,' he admitted. 'We hoped the end might justify the means.'

Cheryl gave up trying to be cross and chuckled instead. 'You know,' she said, 'it's just struck me that you two could make a fortune for yourselves in the Dream Palaces. If you could do it with *anyone*, I mean. Could you?'

'I'm not sure,' Alvin confessed. 'You see we weren't really working *through* you just now. If we had been it would have ended differently.'

'Well, why don't you try the Professor then?' said Cheryl. 'After all, you know her, don't you?'

'Oh I really don't think that –' Professor Poynter started to protest and then, as Cheryl watched, a sort of dreaminess descended upon her. Her head began to move slowly from side to side as though she were following the course of some action visible only to herself. Once or twice she smiled quietly and murmured something in a voice too low for them to catch.

'What's she doing?' Cheryl whispered to the clones.

Alvin glanced at Cheryl. 'Well, maybe you can take a look for yourself,' he said, and as he spoke, Cheryl found herself standing in some sort of steamy changing room surrounded by a dozen naked girls. The illusion lasted no more than a couple of seconds and was never quite as real as her own had been. She blinked her eyes and found that Professor Poynter was back with them again. 'Where was that?' she asked.

'Um?' murmured the Professor.

'That place I saw just now. It was a changing room, wasn't it?'

'The *Amazons* at Cambridge, my dear. Some of my happiest moments were spent between those four walls.'

'We just couldn't hold it for the two of you,' explained Alvin. 'Maybe that was because we had to draw it out of her. But we're beginning to get the hang of things now. Would you like us to try with you again?'

'No,' said Cheryl firmly. 'Thanks all the same.'

29

THAT VERY SAME evening Colin, the third of the clones, was superintending an electronic fish-gutter at the *Kodstaak* processing plant on New Walcheren near the Dutch coast when he became aware that he was no longer alone.

At first, being a romantic youth, he assumed that the beautiful young girl who hovered so tantalizingly in the steamy cloud above the gnashing scissor-grid was a mermaid, and he was moved to utter a cry of warning lest her tail – which was, presumably, veiled by the vapour – should find itself being painfully processed by the hungry blades.

His neighbouring gutter, a chimp called Polderhaas, heard the anguished yelp and came across. He found Colin staring anxiously into the billowing clouds of steam. 'Vot is zer trooble, mine yonk freend?'

Colin turned to him. 'I thought she might get her tail cut off.'

'Ho yerss?' grunted Polderhaas. 'An oo iss zis "she"?'

Colin pointed into the steam. 'Her,' he said. 'The mermaid.'

Polderhaas nodded his head slowly. 'Ow yerss,' he grinned. 'Nice, ent she? Sitch loong blonde 'air an sitch peeg plue ice. Ver' prutty.'

Colin frowned. 'But she's got short brown hair, Polder. And green eyes.'

Polderhaas slapped him on the back and guffawed loudly. 'Too much trinkin', mine freend! You hev ter votch out ze Super don' ketch you et it.'

Colin looked from the chimp to the girl and back again. 'Can't you *see* her, Polder?'

'Ho yerss,' chuckled Polderhas. 'I see 'er goot. Green 'air she got, ent peeg prown ice. Ver' prutty. Smells nice ent fishy too!' and chortling at his own wit he strolled back to his own machine.

Colin watched him go then turned again to the girl. 'What's your name?' he asked gently.

She just smiled at him and said nothing.

'Are you a real mermaid!'

At that instant the steam veils parted a little and the blushing clone observed that the bottom half of her was just as naked as the top. If she had a tail she certainly hadn't brought it with her. She didn't appear to be sitting on anything either. He was just wondering whether he dare risk stretching out a hand and stroking her when, to his bitter disappointment, she dissolved before his very eyes and he was left with only the steam.

For a little while he groped about hoping to locate her, and for the whole of the rest of that shift he was haunted by the thought that she might even now be in the process of being chopped into three-inch cubes, boiled with thermo-nuclear energy, and frozen solid in a series of identical plastic sachets, ready for distribution throughout the Supercities of Europe as *C-FRESH CHUNKY KODLETS*.

At supper in the works' canteen that night Polderhaas started joshing the lad rather heavy-handedly about his mermaid, but Colin's evident distress over the episode soon led to the discussion being diverted into theoretical channels concerning the possible existence and probable physiology of the mermaid as a nautical species. The general consensus of opinion seemed to favour their non-existence, with the rider that if they *did* exist then the likelihood was they would reproduce by spawning. Polderhaas had just started to be very knowledgeable concerning the sex-life of whales when Colin's face was observed to have taken on a look of such fixed and glassy imbecility as was exceptional even for him.

Polderhaas naturally assumed that the clone was rapt in visual contemplation of an organ which he had just described graphically as 'peeg as a toog's funnel' when Colin gulped and uttered the word 'Norbert', adding, a moment later, 'must go and find him. I must, mustn't I?'

'Eh?' enquired the chimp. 'Oo iss Norbert?'

The clone's vacant eyes slowly cleared and he blinked about him in obvious bewilderment.

'You feelin' seek, poy?'

'I saw her,' muttered the amazed clone. 'I saw her again, Polder. Just there!' and he pointed across the table directly at an anthropoid called Oosterbek who had a violent cast in one eye and now grinned at him and touched a finger to his forehead.

'You saw oo?' asked Polderhaas.

'Her,' insisted Colin. 'The one I saw before. Only,' he added in a confidential tone, 'this time she was wearing her clothes.'

The whole problem became instantly clear to Polderhaas. 'Coom, poy,' he said. 'Eat oop. Ve go puy oos som peers down ze Girliehaus. Peeg Margie vill get you shot off zees robbish!'

Colin flushed crimson. 'Oh no, Polder. Really, I couldn't.'

'Sure you kin, poy. Peeg Margie, she poot 'im right, eh Squintz?'

Oosterbek grinned and nodded. 'Sure sure! Gobblim oop!' and

he smacked his lips with a sucking sound.

Colin winced. 'I think I'd rather just go and have a lie down on my bunk, if you don't mind, Polder. I've got an awful headache.'

'I'm vornink you, poy,' said Polderhaas gravely. 'Votch you don' pool 'im ri-toff, or noddinks lef for Peeg Margie or onywan ilse, eh?'

Colin smiled palely, pushed aside his plate, and made his way rather unsteadily out of the mess hall.

He had just left the building and was halfway across the elevated gangway that linked the mess hall to the dormitory block when he suddenly found himself surrounded by a dozen naked girls. The experience was so unsettling that he missed his footing on the slippery concrete and might well have pitched head first into the canal below had he not instinctively grabbed out and caught hold of the metal hand-rail which, to his utter astonishment, seemed to be protruding invisibly from the stomach of one of the nymphs. He clung on to it desperately, shut his eyes, and prayed. When he opened them again the girls were still there busily towelling and powdering themselves and all seemingly oblivious of his presence.

The clone began to whimper and at the same time started to edge his way forward by sliding his hand along the rail which he could no longer see. He had passed completely *through* two of the girls and was advancing upon a third when he heard footsteps approaching. 'Guten Abend, Colin,' cried a cheerful anthropoid voice. 'Vot iss for sopper?' The voice seemed to come out of the air.

'Meat pie,' responded the clone faintly, and became overwhelmingly aware of a pair of rose-pink nipples bouncing around about six inches from his right ear.

'Goot! Meat pie is goot! Wiedersehen!'

'Wiedersehen,' murmured Colin as the invisible footsteps marched briskly past him and faded into the distance. The moment after they had vanished completely, the girls too all suddenly disappeared.

Colin clung to the once-more visible rail as if that too might transform itself into something else. The headache he had pleaded as his excuse for avoiding the Girliehaus was now so intense that he was soon forced to let go of his anchorage and cradle his drumming temples in his palms. As the throbbing eased he took a deep breath and then, very gingerly, proceeded on his way.

Before going to his dormitory he went into the sickbay and asked the duty chimp for a sleeping pill. By the time Polderhaas returned the clone was in a coma so profound that it is doubtful whether even the expert attentions of Big Margie could have aroused him.

30

TWO DAYS LATER, at eleven in the morning Professor Poynter's party, now swollen to five by the addition of a cowled and sandalled monk, jetted in to the Hook of Holland and boarded the hoverbus for New Walcheren. They attracted some curious glances and it was generally assumed that they were members of one of the U.K. Humane Societies which had won themselves an affectionate niche in continental hearts by behaving exactly as the English were always expected to behave, thus perpetuating the ancient legends of Anglo-Saxon eccentricity.

Nevertheless, not all those who watched the Professor shepherd her disparate little flock aboard the bus were convinced that she was going to New Walcheren to investigate the wellbeing of the cod and the halibut. At 21.24 hours the previous evening K.G.3 had finally succeeded in extricating itself from the semantic labyrinth into which it had been led by the appetites of Hortense and the recorded responses of the hapless Pinkerton. An urgent call had gone out alerting all MOSS agents to be on the look out for one elderly female professor, possibly in the company of a middle-aged male anthropoid.

This directive had eventually been relayed to EUROSEC and had actually reached the Hook of Holland an hour before the

Professor landed. Fortunately for her, by one of those annoying little mechanical quirks which were an almost inevitable feature of computerized detection, the message had emerged as a top priority security alert for an elderly female anthropoid and a middle-aged male professor. Since the accompanying stereostills bore little resemblance to their captions a clarification query was despatched to MOSS. By the time the error had been corrected the fugitives had slipped through the net.

Their arrival and departure had, however, been noted by a plain-clothes EUROSEC agent, a chimp named Moesbrooger. This up-and-coming young sleuth had made an inspired guess (one day these would become famous throughout the force as 'Captain Moesbrooger's hunches') that the elderly lady and the middle-aged chimp with her were none other than the objects of the garbled MOSS alert. Acting entirely on his own initiative he had trailed them down to the hoverbus terminal and learnt their destination.

By the time Moesbrooger returned to the EUROSEC office the correction from London had come through and he was able to earn himself a swift commendation by informing his superiors that the quarry they sought was now en route for New Walcheren. This information was shuttled back to MOSS and, within a matter of minutes, the following unequivocal reply had been received: 'UU+⁎⁎ D.W.P.F.F.Q.⁎⁎ MOSS-LOND'. Translated from international code this message read, '*Most urgent. Detain whole party forthwith for questioning.*'

Fifteen minutes later a coal black 'Thunderbird' helicopter with silver EUROSEC markings, rose like a pregnant locust above the dykes and polders, cocked its tail and headed out to sea.

The Professor's party were already inside the *Kodstaak* complex when their pursuers came racing in over the slate grey wastes of the North Sea, made a brisk circuit of the artificial island and settled to a squat on the flat roof of the Packing Department which served the factory as a landing ground. Out climbed a EUROSEC lieutenant, a sergeant, and Moesbrooger. They conferred briefly then headed for the elevator access.

At that moment Professor Poynter finally succeeded in convincing the *Kodstaak* Personnel Manager that she had not come to enquire into the company's dubious methods of dispatching its raw material. At once he ceased to be obstructive and offered to conduct them himself to the Processing plant where, he assured them, young Colin would just be beginning his mid-morning shift. The Professor thanked him and the party trooped out of the office and down the passage.

They entered the Processing plant from one end just as their pursuers entered it from the other, but both parties were initially concealed from one another by the clouds of fishy steam which effectively reduced visibility to rather less than twenty yards. While Cheryl, Norbert and the Professor peered about them seeking for a replica of Alvin and Bruce, the two inner-directed clones simply pointed ahead and said: 'There he is.'

The words were hardly uttered before one of the misty shapes ahead of them lurched backwards, staggered in the aisle and clasped its head in its overalled arms. As they hurried forward it regained its balance, slowly straightened up and turned towards them.

'Is he all right?' enquired Cheryl anxiously.

'He's fine,' Bruce assured her. 'He picked us up the night before last apparently and that took the edge off it.'

The third clone came towards them, regarded them thoughtfully for a moment and then grinned. 'Hello,' he said. 'Where's the rest of us?'

'Somewhere in Africa,' said Alvin. 'We're on our way to pick him up.'

'Professor Poynter?' enquired an unfamiliar voice.

They all looked up and found themselves confronted by two uniformed EUROSEC officers, a *Kodstaak* receptionist (human), and an ape in civilian clothes.

'Yes, I am Professor Poynter.'

The Lieutenant slipped a hand inside his tunic and produced a photoprint warrant card. 'I represent EUROSEC, madam. I'm afraid I must ask you and your party to return with me to Rotterdam.'

The Professor gave a rather unconvincing imitation of a light-hearted laugh. 'But there must be some mistake, officer.'

None knew better than the minions of EUROSEC just how likely *that* was, but at least their warrant ensured that they wouldn't be the ones to catch any rebounds if she was right. 'We have a helicopter waiting, madam,' said the Lieutenant. 'You will all come with us, please.'

'And if we refuse?'

'That would be most unwise.'

'Do you mean you're arresting us?'

'I am merely carrying out my orders, madam.'

'Orders from whom, may I ask?'

'MOSS in London.'

Professor Poynter's infant hopes were butchered and buried. She looked round at the three clones and her eyes filled with tears. 'Forgive me,' she murmured. 'It was too much to hope.'

Alvin, Bruce and Colin regarded her in triplicated wonder while, like a flickering shuttle, soundless questions and answers darted back and forth between them.

— *What's she on about?*

— *Who's MOSS?*

— *She's a decent old cow.*

— *How the hell are we going to make it to Africa now?*

— *Any of us fly a 'copter?*

— *We can try.*

— *We'll have to ditch this lot first.*

— *How?*

— *Easy. Get ours over to this side.*

Without consciously deciding to do so Cheryl, Norbert and the Professor found they had taken four paces to the left and were standing side by side with their backs pressed to the long wall which faced the processors. The three clones tagged themselves on to the end of the line, leaving only the *Kodstaak* Personnel Manager confronting the mystified EUROSEC team. There was a pause of not more than a couple of seconds, then the astounded security men saw their quarry dart forward and dive, one after the other, head first into the scissor-grids.

So utterly unexpected was this mass immolation that for some moments Moesbrooger and his companions were completely paralysed. The Personnel Manager was the first to react. Leaping forward he clawed at the 'Emergency Stop' button and brought the processor to a clattering, hissing halt.

The witnesses of the tragedy crowded round him and peered aghast into the steamy bowels of the machine. 'What will have happened to them?' whispered the horrified Lieutenant.

The Personnel Manager whisked a finger rapidly back and forth across his throat. 'Quickly!' he gasped. 'At all costs we must prevent their getting fed into Packaging!'

As their racing footsteps died away six concrete buttresses appeared to detach themselves from the wall where the Professor's party had been standing.

'How long do you think we've got?' asked one.

'Not more than ten minutes,' said another.

'Where's this plane?' asked the third.

'On the roof. We can take the lift from Reception.'

Whereupon the six buttresses metamorphosed into three identical clones, two human females and one extremely puzzled anthropoid.

'Quick!' said Colin. 'It won't take them long to discover we aren't there.'

Three minutes later they emerged on the roof of the Packing Department. The helicopter was standing where the EUROSEC pilot had left it. There was no one in sight. 'Try and look as though we own it,' said Colin.

The clones scrambled aboard and dragged the others in after them. 'Surely one of us must have read how you fly these things,' said Alvin. 'Come on now. *Think!*'

'This any use?' suggested Bruce and there, hovering in the air before them was a volume entitled: *The Bright Boy's Book of World Aircraft*. The pages riffled over. Veetols, airships, sailplanes, balloons, helicopters of every conceivable variety, but not a word on how one actually *flew* any one of them.

'How about this?' said Alvin. The book vanished and was replaced by a screen on which Captain Fortitude, a So-Vi serial hero, was crouched in the cockpit of his helicar and diving down upon some fleeing malefactors.

'Go back and see if it shows him starting it up,' said Colin.

The phantom So-Vi screen went into swift reverse, then the picture cut to a close-up of the crooks' speeding aquaplane. The clones swore.

'Here,' said Cheryl. 'Move over. Let me have a go.'

Alvin vacated the pilot's seat. She lowered herself into it, peered at the instruments before her, and then nodded. 'Do you want me to have a try?'

'What have we got to lose?' sighed the Professor.

'Our lives maybe,' grinned Cheryl and thumbed a green button hopefully. There was a combustive cough from somewhere above them and they all felt the machine begin to tremble. 'Now pray!' commanded Cheryl. '*Hard!*' and eased back the control column.

31

IN ASSUMING THAT their pursuers would require only ten minutes to discover they had been hoodwinked, the clones had seriously underestimated their own powers. To their dying day four humans and one anthropoid were prepared to swear on oath that they had seen Professor Poynter and her companions leap to their deaths in a fish processor. They spent just over one and a half hours trying to locate what was left of the bodies and it was not until the Personnel Manager thought to question the other workers in the Processing plant that they learnt, incredulously, how, shortly after they themselves had quit the building, a party of visitors guided by young Colin had been seen making its way towards Reception. At this point Moesbrooger had his second brilliant hunch in one day. 'The 'copter!' he grunted.

They reached the empty roof of the Packing Department just five minutes after a EUROSEC 'Thunderbird', apparently containing six uniformed EUROSEC officers, had touched down at Stuttgart, taken aboard a full load of fuel and departed in a south-easterly direction for an unspecified destination.

By the time Moesbrooger's party had agreed on their story, phoned in their report to Rotterdam, been disbelieved, and had finally succeeded in convincing their superiors that they had not gone corporately mad, Cheryl was gunning merrily along in the purloined machine a thousand metres above the Gulf of Rapallo en route for Sardinia.

As Corsica came in sight the three clones let out a shrill cheer.

'What's that in aid of?' asked Cheryl, turning to them in some surprise.

'Desmond,' they said. 'We've just made contact with him.'

'Protein for you,' she grunted. 'Be sure to give him my fond regards.'

'He's really looking forward to meeting you, Cheryl. We've told him about you.'

'And have you told him what a fix we're in?' she enquired. 'I'm not sure what the penalty is for nicking one of these things but I suspect it's likely to be pretty sensational.'

'Don't you worry about that,' they assured her. 'We can fix it now, easily.'

'If you're hoping to get away with that Stuttgart trick in Cagliari, you'd better think again. I'll bet they've alerted the whole of Europe by this time.'

'They have,' said Norbert who had been experimenting with the communications. 'They've just broadcast our description as a Red Plus alert on all bands. They say we've disguised ourselves as international police and are armed to the teeth.'

'You're sure they didn't say *with* teeth?' queried Cheryl sardonically. 'What are we supposed to be? Bank robbers?'

'U.A.B. guerrillas,' said Norbert, adding with a grin, 'They say I'm the master-mind behind the whole operation.'

Cheryl gave an indignant yelp. '*Piker!* Trust that cheap skate to jump on the bandwagon! Have they identified us yet?'

'Only me and the Professor so far,' said Norbert.

Cheryl glanced at the airspeed indicator. 'At this rate we'll be at Cagliari inside an hour and I don't speak two words of Italian. If anyone's got any bright suggestions let's have them.'

'Just leave it to us,' said Alvin. 'You put us down as far from the control tower as you can, taxi us up to the fuel point and we'll look after the rest.'

'Including the couple of hundred trigger-happy flics who'll be out to avenge the honour of EUROSEC?'

Alvin grinned. 'I don't suppose there'll be that many. But don't worry anyway.'

'I've always admired self-confidence,' muttered Cheryl, 'but this is ridiculous.'

Alvin, Bruce and Colin became one vast, smug grin.

It was the dead hour of the afternoon when Julius Augustino Peccavi, junior Flight Control Officer at Cagliari heliport, alone on duty in the observation tower, perceived on his scanner screen the blip of an unknown aircraft approaching from the north. He formally requested it to identify itself and was informed, in very curious Italian, that the visitor was none other than His Holiness – *Il Papa*.

Just to be on the safe side, Julius Augustino crossed himself before requesting further confirmation. He received in return a quavering blessing in the name of the Father, the Son and the Holy Spirit. At this point the blip vanished from the screen.

Not entirely convinced, Peccavi left his post, walked across to the window that gave a wide view over the whole airfield, and gazed out. No sign of any strange aircraft could he see. In fact the only moving object in sight was a tanker-truck making its way round the perimeter towards the fuel depot. He watched as it drew up alongside a fuel point, saw a blue-overalled figure descend from the cab, swing out the pump jib, connect up the hose and then return to work the controls.

Julius Augustino stroked his moustache and felt curiously uneasy. Had he imagined that blip? *Non posso!* Then where was the aircraft that had caused it? Returning to his seat he slipped on his headphones and thumbed the recall/record button. The extraordinary identification signal was there all right, mixed up with some strange atmospheric interference that sounded remarkably like girlish giggling – a sound pattern upon which the Flight Controller had every right to consider himself an authority.

While he was still puzzling over the mystery his scanner picked up a second blip. Julius Augustino frowned and once again transmitted the official identification demand. 'EUROSEC PY 0117,' came the swift, no-nonsense reply. 'Request permission to land and re-fuel.'

Peccavi's dark eyes gleamed with excitement. 'Come in EUROSEC,' he said. 'All clear for touch down,' and while he was still speaking he was pressing his thumb down hard on the red alert button.

From their hiding places in the hangars round the terminal swarthy-faced security agents crept forward, peered up at the Sardinian sky, and fingered their lasers and their gas guns. The honour of EUROSEC was in their hands. '*Mama mia*,' they prayed silently. 'Let me be the one.'

Julius Augustino watched the blip drift off the screen then he raced to the window. Level with his eyes a black and silver 'Thunderbird' was hovering prior to settling. On the oil-smudged concrete below all was tranquil. He squinted into the helicopter's cabin and counted one, two, three, four heads. Should there not have been more? Five? or was it six? The machine's shadow was darting in to meet it. 'Eager as a lover,' thought the romantic Flight Controller. Shadow and substance fused, became one. The twinkling rotor blades slowed, clicked, were still. '*Pronto! Pronto!*' begged Julius Augustino, hopping from one foot to the other in his excitement.

Precisely according to prearranged plan a tanker rolled forward and came to stop alongside the aircraft. A EUROSEC agent disguised as a mechanic jumped down and ran forward with the hose. The gleaming nozzle was locked home. The pseudo-mechanic raised his left arm and, in an eye-blink the aircraft was surrounded.

The cockpit door flew open and from inside a startled face peered out just in time to catch the full blast of a gas gun. '*Bravo! Bravissimo!*' applauded Julius Augustino as the villain sagged insensible from the cockpit.

Meanwhile, unobserved, the tanker-truck which Peccavi had been watching five minutes before, had now left the fuel point and made its way to the southernmost corner of the airfield, far away from the scene of all the excitement. It rolled to a stop in the dark shadow of an air-freight depository. A minute later, just as the last of the unconscious officers was being hauled unceremoniously from the cabin of one EUROSEC 'Thunderbird', another rose from behind the air-freight building, slanted up into the declining sun and disappeared out to sea. The only people who took more than a cursory interest in its departure were two young children who ran home and told their mother they had just seen a lorry change into a helicopter. Each was very properly rewarded with a sound slap for telling such wicked lies.

32

THE SOLAR POWER-STATION at Umm el Raha differed hardly at all from the thousand others scattered along the 25th parallel and which collectively made up the Sahara Grid. It consisted of 750 sun-seeking parabolic mirrors, each thirty feet in diameter, which employed the Balchover thermo-couple to convert 37% of the concentrated solar heat directly into electrical energy. Some 2% of this power was utilized to drive the motors which guided the aluminized fibreglass dishes and the rest was fed directly into the Grid. The mirrors – known universally as 'sunflowers' – were planted on their slender stalks in a fenced 'garden' roughly five hundred yards square. At one corner of the 'garden' was the 'greenhouse' from which the collected current was piped away, and in another was the 'toolshed' where the technicians lived. All these objects had other names in English, French and Arabic, and all the names were obscene.

Apart from the engineer overseers who were stationed in the relative comfort of places like Sebha and In Salah, the Sahara Grid was staffed entirely by apes. Umm el Raha was the one exception. It was also a leading contender for the title of 'Backside of the Universe'. Its annual rainfall had once been assessed at .01 cm. per annum, and that was in a wet year. Its last prickly shrub had been gnawed to death by a suicidal goat in 1853 and since then nothing else had dared to put down a root. Its landscape made the words 'harsh' and 'barren' seem almost pastoral. To gaze out over those endless quivering miles of reddish-grey desolation shrivelled the heart and dried the spittle in the throat. The only creatures which were able to survive unaided were the flies. Locusts had long since given up Umm el Raha as hopeless.

The unannounced descent upon the plateau at 16.30 hours (international time) of two EUROSEC rocket shuttles was at first ascribed to some hitherto unknown form of mirage, but as the

144

dust settled and the ports opened and twelve armed and uniformed humans leapt out and began sprinting towards the station, the astonished staff of Umm el Raha realized that something altogether extraordinary was taking place. They were right.

At 14.30 hours the news of what had happened at New Walcheren, Stuttgart and Cagliari had been fed into OMEGA the EUROSEC master computer. OMEGA had been coupled with the K.G.3 computer at MOSS which had just finished digesting the report from Saint Clumbert's and tying this in with all it had so far assimilated of the Poynter investigation. The resultant diagnosis was so spectacularly improbable that at first no one would believe it and precious time was lost while the security software was frantically re-checked.

At 15.00 hours the heads of ten European states, summoned to an emergency stereo-So-Vi conference, heard the suave voice of OMEGA announce that humanity was facing a challenge without parallel in its history – nothing less than the advent of a suprahuman species of virtually incalculable powers. There followed a recorded interview with a blandly unrepentant Sir Gordon Loveridge and a brief transmission of selected extracts from the M.O.P. video-tape of Miriam Poynter's first confrontation with the corporate clones. When it was concluded, Herr Buber, the President of The Council of Ten, asked the members collectively for their opinion on what action should be taken.

Monsieur Traubert, the French Premier, had no doubts on the matter. He expressed himself as usual with characteristic Gallic pungency. 'Mais c'est simple, Messieurs! Isolation: Incarceration: Extermination!'

Herr Buber proceeded to put the question individually to the rest. When they had all expressed an opinion he called for a formal vote. Six members agreed with M. Traubert; one – Mr O'Duffy – disagreed; and three abstained on grounds of principle (unspecified) which were privately assumed to have some connection with French agricultural policy.

The decision having been taken it only remained to entrust EUROSEC with the job of carrying out the sentence before the Human Righters got wind of it and started lodging an appeal with the World Court. OMEGA was consulted as to the best method of proceeding. It advised the immediate destruction of the surviving genetic material in the M.O.P. vaults and the summary liquidation of the fourth clone before reunification could be effected. It added that it was by no means certain whether the latter was now possible. The despatching of the two military rocket shuttles to Umm el Raha was the prompt initiation of Phase One, *'Opération Déraciner'*.

Speed and surprise, as Clausewitz shrewdly observed, are excellent ingredients for a successful military operation, and so far as the astounded anthropoids at Umm el Raha were concerned EUROSEC undoubtedly achieved both. Within two minutes of the rockets' touch down the apes found themselves herded into the dining hall and lined up against a wall. The Colonel in charge of the operation strode in and slapped his dusty jackboot with a neural probe. 'Well?' he growled. 'Where is he?'

The chimps glanced at each other out of the corners of their eyes. 'Where is who, *effendi*?' enquired Abdullah, the Station Foreman, cautiously.

'Desmond,' hissed the Colonel.

There was a perceptible letting out of anthropoid breath. Although they were all fond of the clone they were, understandably, even fonder of their own skins. Abdullah peered along the line and then shrugged. 'I do not know, *effendi*. Perhaps with his tomato plants?'

'Comb the place,' ordered the Colonel. 'Every centimetre! *He must be found!*'

The soldiers ran out leaving their chief to stride tigerishly up and down the line of trembling apes, muttering to himself and whisking an invisible tail.

In ten minutes they were back and the Colonel learnt that the clone had apparently vanished into the dust. His rage and frustration were beyond belief. Apes and humans alike regarded him with awed apprehension.

'Make an announcement through the loud-hailer, Schulze,' he snarled. 'Say we will shoot one ape at intervals of five minutes until he gives himself up!'

'Ja, Herr Kolonel!'

'Correction!' snapped the Colonel. 'One every *three* minutes!'

'Ja, Herr Kolonel. Every *three* minutes.' The Sergeant saluted and hurried out.

The Colonel brooded along the ranged and quaking chimps like a Bavarian thundercloud. He paused before a plainly pregnant young female. 'You,' he demanded sombrely. 'What is your name?'

'Scherezade,' she whispered.

'So,' grunted the Colonel, and turning to one of his soldiers said: 'Tell Schulze to announce that Scherezade will be the first to be shot.'

A young male chimp flung himself forward on his knees and clutched at the Colonel's boots. 'Not her!' he cried. 'Please, sir, not her! Shoot me!'

The Colonel was not entirely devoid of compassion. 'By all means,' he said. 'You shall be the next.'

The bead curtains which concealed the passageway to the kitchens parted and in strolled Desmond. 'Hello,' he said. 'What's going on?'

The Colonel who had just drawn back his leg to boot the supplicant into line swung round and caught sight of the clone. 'So!' he cried. 'You have come at last!'

Desmond blinked and brushed a lethargic fly from his burnous. 'Colonel Potzdammer?' he enquired.

'*You know who I am?*'

The clone nodded. 'I've been expecting you for the last hour.'

At that moment Sergeant Schulze's voice boomed out over the station informing the empty desert that Scherezade was to be executed in three minutes' time.

'That will not be necessary,' the Colonel informed the relieved apes. 'You may go. We have the man we want.'

The words were scarcely pronounced before the chimps had scuttled away leaving Desmond alone in the hall to face Colonel Potzdammer and his troopers.

The Colonel consulted his timeteller and signalled to two of his men to seize the clone. 'It is of little consequence,' he said, 'but I am curious to know how you learnt of my name.'

Desmond laughed. 'I doubt if you would understand if I told you, Colonel.'

The Colonel shrugged. 'Very well,' he said. 'Then I assume you also know why we are here?'

Desmond nodded.

The Colonel regarded him with renewed interest. 'Tell me,' he commanded.

'Well, to kill me, of course.'

'Quite correct,' said the Colonel.

'It was not a very difficult deduction.'

'You are not afraid to die?'

The clone smiled.

'Remarkable,' murmured the Colonel.

'And what makes you so sure you *can* kill me, Colonel?'

Colonel Potzdammer laughed ferociously. 'That we shall demonstrate in two minutes from now. Personally I have no doubts whatsoever on the matter. Shall we proceed?'

Escorted by a soldier at either side Desmond was marched out on to the blistering plateau and placed with his back to a lump of rock. Eight troopers took up their positions ten metres away from him and unslung their guns. Sergeant Schulze peered through the viewfinder of his camera and hummed an air from *Turandot*. The two men who had acted as prisoner's escort stepped smartly aside and joined on at either end of the firing squad. Colonel Potzdammer lifted his probe like a conductor's baton. 'Eins!' he said crisply. 'Zwei! Drei!' The probe swished down.

Ten lethal laser beams skeined the shimmering air like strands of sapphire silk.

And the clone vanished.

33

THE SUN WAS an enormous crimson globe balanced upon the black seal's snout of distant Mount Ahaggar when Cheryl brought the helicopter drifting down among the scattered stones which were all that now remained of the ancient palace of the Mighty Kings of Zub.

The fugitives clambered out, rubbing their aching muscles. 'Are you *sure* this is right?' asked Cheryl peering up doubtfully at a ruined ziggaraut which, four thousand years before, had been one of the wonders of its ancient world.

The clones conferred briefly and then nodded.

'Where's Desmond then?'

'He's coming,' they assured her. 'He won't be long now.'

'Well, I don't know about anyone else,' she said, 'but I'm dying for a pee.' With that she set off across what had once been the bridal chamber of a Queen of Queens but was now only a shallow rectangular depression in a waste of silvery sand.

The shadows stretched themselves out like waking cats and turned from mauve to purple. The cooling desert creaked and whispered.

'This is a strange place, ma'am,' said Norbert gazing round at the wind polished stumps of marble columns which the declining sun was rinsing in a rose-pink wash of almost unbelievable delicacy. 'Remarkably peaceful.'

Professor Poynter nodded. ' "Then on the shore," ' she murmured,

' "Of the wide world I stand alone, and think
Till death and fame to nothingness do sink." '

' "*Love*" ' whispered a voice in her ear. ' "Till *love* and fame to nothingness do sink." '

She jerked round and there was nobody there.

'How very odd,' she said. 'I could have sworn . . .'

She looked across at the three clones. They had scratched out an equilateral triangle in the sand and were now sitting cross-legged, one at each corner. They appeared to be just staring blankly at one another.

'Norbert?' she enquired. 'Did *you* hear anything?'

'Ma'am?'

'A voice whispering.'

Norbert cocked his head on one side and listened. 'No, ma'am,' he said.

'I must be getting old,' she thought.

'Nonsense,' said the voice. 'You know very well you're in the prime of life.'

'Oh, do be quiet,' she said.

'I beg your pardon, ma'am,' Norbert apologized. 'A touch of wind.'

'Not you, Norbert. *It*.'

' "It", ma'am?'

'Well, *really*,' said the voice plaintively. ' "It", indeed! Whatever next?'

Cheryl emerged from her place of concealment, clambered up on to a pile of stones and waved to them.

Norbert waved back and then he and the Professor started walking to meet her. When they had covered half the distance Norbert paused, looked about him, and shook his head. 'This place reminds me of somewhere,' he said, 'and yet I don't see how it can. What did they call it? Zug?'

'Zub,' said the Professor. 'They maintain it has some obscure meaning in Ancient Persian. Considering that we are now somewhere in the middle of Libya I must say that seems highly unlikely.'

Cheryl did a tightrope-walker's balancing act, ran along the top of a half-buried wall, jumped down and came to join them. 'This place is *weird*,' she said.

'What do you mean?' asked the Professor.

Cheryl rubbed her nose with the back of her hand. 'Well, over there,' she said, 'just as I was climbing up those stones I could have sworn I heard birds singing. I ask you – birds in this place! You can't have *sound* mirages, can you?'

'I don't know,' said the Professor. 'I don't *think* you can.'

'You don't suppose *they* might have had something to do with it?'

The three of them turned and contemplated the immobile clones.

'What on earth are they up to now?' asked Cheryl. 'Holding a prayer meeting?'

'Nothing would surprise me,' said the Professor. 'They've long since passed beyond the bounds of my comprehension.'

'You can say *that* again,' murmured Cheryl. 'If I hadn't met Alvin the way I did, quite frankly they'd scare me stiff. Now all I'm doing is crossing my fingers and hoping they know what they're up to.'

Norbert nodded sagely. 'All they ask of us is that we trust them.'

'They've told you that?' enquired Cheryl curiously.

'Not in so many words,' said Norbert. 'But I'm sure it's true.'

Cheryl stirred the sand with her toe. 'When you first thought of making them, Miriam, did you have any idea *what* you were doing! – apart from breaking the law, I mean.'

'No, not really,' admitted the Professor. 'It just seemed a rather fascinating piece of research.'

'It didn't – well, ever *worry* you?'

'Ethically, you mean?'

'Yes, I suppose I do.'

'No, I can't say that it did. Of course I made sure Sir Gordon was kept informed.'

'But didn't you ever say to yourself – "Here are four living breathing human beings which but for me would never have existed"?'

The Professor smiled indulgently. 'Oh, no,' she said. 'That's not the way we think at the M.O.P.'

'But you do still feel responsible for them, don't you?'

'I certainly *did*,' admitted the Professor. 'I now hope they feel responsible for *me*.'

'Come again?'

'Well, it's quite obvious they have no further *need* of me.'

'But that goes for all of us,' said Cheryl. 'We've got them together again and now, presumably, they'll discard us and move on to higher things – whatever *they* are.'

'Pardon me, Miss Cheryl,' interposed Norbert, 'I don't believe that could be their intention at all.'

'No?' said Cheryl, regarding the ape in some surprise. 'Have I missed something?'

'We should not make the mistake of judging them by our own worldly standards, Miss,' said the chimp deferentially. 'I cannot as yet speak for Master Colin or Master Desmond, but Alvin and Bruce have qualities of saintliness that would put ordinary mortals to shame.'

Cheryl blinked and then grinned. 'Maybe you're right at that, Norbert,' she said. 'I'm quite sure *I've* never met anything like them.'

'No one has,' said the Professor. 'They are absolutely unique.

The first genuinely gestalt human personality the world has ever known.'

'Is that good or bad?' asked Cheryl. 'Or is that another ethical question?'

'It is certainly not one *I* feel qualified to answer,' replied the Professor.

Cheryl eyed her thoughtfully. 'Do *you* believe what they said about EUROSEC trying to kill Desmond?'

'I have no reason to *dis*believe it.'

'Then that must mean that the Government thinks they *are* bad, mustn't it?'

'An excellent argument for believing that they're *good*,' said the Professor grimly.

'Protein for you, Professor!' cried Cheryl slapping her on the back. 'Ask me for a phoney and I'll show you a politician!'

Professor Poynter flushed faintly. 'But isn't your father . . . ?'

'Oh, he's typical,' said Cheryl. 'Mind you, I don't think he'd have gone so far as actually *killing* them. He'd probably have wanted to float them as a company with himself as major shareholder. On the whole,' she concluded judiciously, 'the killing would probably have been a cleaner death.'

By now the sun had slipped right down behind the distant mountains leaving an orange glow on the western horizon. This shaded off through yellow-green into amethyst, and finally into deepest indigo through which the first stars were beginning to prick their way. As the shadows darkened among the ruins the air immediately surrounding the three silent clones became subtly luminous until they appeared to be enclosed within a fragile hemisphere of trembling, pale blue light.

As the others approached, this hemisphere expanded outwards and upwards until it was occupying an area roughly ten yards in diameter. Overcome by curiosity Cheryl stepped forward and stretched out her hand. 'Hey!' she exclaimed. 'This thing's *real*! *Solid!*'

As she was speaking the dome edged outwards another couple of feet and she found herself being pushed gently but firmly backwards. She felt extremely surprised and, truth to tell, a little hurt, for she was not a girl who took kindly to being excluded from anything. She sat down on the sand and braced her back against the dome, only to find herself being quietly bulldozed along on her bottom as the hemisphere drew in yet another breath and puffed itself up some more.

As soon as she had come to rest she burrowed her fingers down into the sand and discovered to her astonishment that the dome continued underground. She pressed her nose up against the transparent surface and peered in like a child squinting through a sweetshop window. 'Hi, there!' she called. 'You inside! What's going on?'

If the clones heard her they certainly gave no sign. In fact, as far as she could judge, they hadn't moved an inch. Furthermore they didn't even appear to be *breathing*!

Cheryl gave a disgusted snort, climbed up off her knees and slapped the sand from the seat of her tunic. 'That's gratitude for you,' she grumbled. 'Risk your neck flying them out into the middle of nowhere and what thanks do you get? What are we supposed to do? Freeze quietly to death? Besides, I'm starving.'

'There are some emergency rations in the helicopter, Miss,' observed Norbert.

Cheryl brightened immediately. 'Why didn't you say so before?' she cried. 'Come on, chimp!'

The three of them turned their backs on the mysterious, glimmering dome and set off towards the helicopter. By so doing they effectively deprived themselves of a unique opportunity to witness the transcendental advent of a teleported clone. He arrived, complete with white burnous, some ten seconds after they had left the scene. His point of materialization was both the precise epicentre of the transparent sphere and the exact locus of the equilateral triangle.

34

At 18.30 hours the ten European Chiefs of State were once again summarily convened and informed, first by their President and then by General Pretzel, the Head of EURO-SEC, of what had taken place at Umm el Raha. Naturally none of them believed it. They were then shown Sergeant Schulze's filmed record of Desmond's execution, together with a commentary supplied by Colonel Potzdammer, and ten fertile seeds of doubt were planted.

'Colonel Potzdammer is absolutely trustworthy, gentlemen,' said General Pretzel. 'That is why he was selected for this particular mission. He has tendered me his resignation, which, naturally, I have refused to accept.'

The Council of Ten nodded collectively to signify their approval.

'An' what do we do now?' enquired the amiable Mr O'Duffy. 'Exorcise de spot?'

' "Exercise le sport"?' queried the French Premier elevating the famous Traubert eyebrows. 'Quoi? Expliquez moi.'

'Exorcise,' repeated Mr O'Duffy. 'Sprinkle around de holy water an' what not.'

'Ah, exorciser! Je comprehends. C'est une plaisanterie ir-landaise. Ho ho!'

'If you've got a better suggestion me boyo, let's be afther havin' it.'

Herr Buber decided to intervene. 'Since receiving Colonel Potzdammer's report we have succeeded in locating the stolen helicopter. If you please, General.'

A map of North Africa appeared on the ministerial So-Vi screens of Dublin, London, Berlin, etc. General Pretzel tapped it with his swagger stick. 'Here, gentlemen,' he said, 'is Umm el Raha, and here' – moving the point some two hundred scale miles westward – 'is the helicopter. It has come down in the middle of the desert, having, presumably, run out of fuel before it could reach its destination.'

'Smart work, General,' said Sir Peter Whiplash. 'Congratulations.'

General Pretzel touched his moustache with the tip of his cane in discreet acknowledgement of the compliment. 'As far as we can tell,' he said, 'the occupants are still in the immediate vicinity.'

'Alors? Que'est-ce que nous attendons?'

'Might we remind Monsieur Traubert that the language of this assembly is officially English?' said Sir Peter.

'*Pardon!*' M. Traubert writhed his lips in a bitter smile. 'I ask vot are ve vating for? You understand, Sir Peter?'

'Oh, rather!' said Sir Peter genially. 'Just protocol, you understand. Nothing personal. Myself I'm happy to parlay fronsay any time.'

Herr Buber coughed. 'There would appear to be two answers to Monsieur Traubert's question. The first is that Libya happens to be situated in North Africa and not in Europe. The second is that OMEGA has advised proceeding with extreme caution.'

'Still, that didn't stop Potzdammer having a go, did it?'

'No, Sir Peter. But there we were taking a calculated risk on both counts. The Libyan attaché was informed the moment we learned that Colonel Potzdammer's mission had failed.'

'Oh, yes?' said Sir Peter. 'How did he take it?'

'Diplomatically.'

'An' how about de other fella?' enquired the Irish Premier.

'You are referring to OMEGA, Mr O'Duffy?'

'That's right.'

'The computer's reaction is less easy to summarize. In the circumstances I thought it advisable to arrange for you all to put your questions to it directly. Do I have your permission?'

Nobody objected and the closed circuit was accordingly let out a further notch to include the pride and joy of European Security. 'Good evening, gentlemen,' it said. 'Can I assist you?'

'You've heard what happened at Umm el Raha, I suppose?' said Sir Peter.

The computer remained silent.

'Well, have you or haven't you?'

'Yes,' said OMEGA. 'Of course I have.'

'Well, what do you make of it?'

'You wish for an explanation of the phenomenon of teleportation?'

'Tele-*what*?'

'Teleportation. Derived from the Greek *tele* – "far off" or "distant" – and the Latin *portare* – "to carry". Hence "carry far off". Teleport.'

'Well, I'm damned,' said Sir Peter. 'You mean it actually *happens*?'

'So it would appear,' said the computer.

'Well, what do we do about it?'

'You wish to experience the phenomenon for yourself?'

'Good Lord, no! I mean what do *we* do? How do we cope with these – what-d'you-call-its? – clones? Dammit, they might pop up anywhere!'

'I am inclined to believe that it is now too late to do anything about it. The events at Umm el Raha have merely confirmed my earlier analysis. Extrapolation suggests that further moves of a similar nature may well provoke unforeseeable consequences.'

'Are you trying to tell us that these chaps really *are* dangerous?'

'Insofar as all superior life forms present a threat to all inferior life forms, that is certainly true.'

'But vat could zey do?' asked M. Traubert. '*Kill* us?'

'Undoubtedly.'

'Then why didn't they kill Potzdammer?' demanded Sir Peter.

'Presumably because they chose not to. As a demonstration of their power, what they achieved was equally effective.'

Signor Umberto now spoke for the first time. 'You say the other three are at present in the desert?'

'I have been given this information,' said OMEGA. 'I have not cross-checked it.'

'It's true all right,' said General Pretzel. 'Sky Bird picked them up and we've identified the aircraft.'

'*Bene*,' said Signor Umberto. 'They are now in the desert. By now, I assume, we have their precise co-ordinates. We also have Vulture intercontinental thermo-nuclear missiles in Malta and Cyprus. Do I make myself clear, gentlemen?'

'Ah sure now,' said Mr O'Duffy, 'isn't that goin' from one extreme to th'other? These fellas haven't hurt anyone. All they've done is hijack a helicopter. Sure you can't atomize them just fer that!'

'And what do *you* suggest, Mr O'Duffy?'

'Well, less at least *talk* to them or somethin'. Ask 'em t'give 'emselves up. Thass only fair. Besides, I don't suppose the Libyans would take so kindly to us poopin' off our Vultures into their desert wi'out so much as a by-your-leave.'

'You have heard OMEGA's assessment of their potential, Mr O'Duffy,' said Herr Buber. 'The threat they pose is in every sense a real one.'

'So *he* says,' said Mr O'Duffy. 'Sure he's just a bunch o' wires.'

'Ovonics,' corrected OMEGA primly.

'Well, I still don't see what we stand to lose by jist *talkin'* to them,' protested O'Duffy.

'You lose the element of surprise,' said the computer.

'Ah, why don't you go an' fuse yeself,' muttered the Prime Minister of God's Own Country.

The discussion continued for a further forty minutes and then Signor Umberto's proposal was put to the vote. Five supported the motion and five opposed it. Whereupon Herr Buber communed with his conscience and decided, with some misgiving, that, in the interests of inferior humanity, all that remained of the Ancient Palace of the Once Mighty Kings of Zub should forthwith be blasted back into the dust from which it had arisen.

Just as he was about to announce on which side he had cast his vote, there was a sort of gurgling gulp from the computer and there, blinking out from ten Prime Ministerial stereo-So-Vi screens in ten different European capitals, were those amiable booby features which Nature in her inscrutable wisdom had selected for the next great leap forward of the human species. Was the face Alvin's or Colin's or Bruce's or Desmond's? The question was no longer meaningful. It was simply the face of the clone.

'Gentlemen,' it said, and each Head of State heard himself being addressed in his own mother tongue, 'I must ask you to forgive this intrusion which, I assure you, I had hoped would prove unnecessary. I am here only to prevent you from committing a grave error of judgement. Your computer has pronounced me to be a threat to humanity – a verdict which, within its own terms of reference, is certainly justifiable. But what it has understandably overlooked is that, in my own case, its terms of reference can no longer be held to apply. The ant cannot pass meaningful judgement upon the eagle for they belong to different species. The wisdom of the one is not the wisdom of the other.

'Nevertheless, from one point of view, your computer's assessment has undeniable substance. I do indeed constitute a threat to you, but this threat comes not from *me*, but from yourselves. You cannot destroy me, but in attempting to do so you will assuredly destroy humanity. Since I have no wish to annihilate either you personally or the society which you represent, I will explain briefly what steps I intend to take in the event of your proceeding with your present plan. When I have concluded I will ask you to put the question once more to your computer. My hope is that though you may not believe *me*, you will be prepared to accept the advice of an impartial, logical intelligence whose reasoning processes are modelled upon your own.'

The clone paused and seemed to gaze directly into their uneasy hearts. 'You intend to launch a Vulture missile strike against me from Malta and Cyprus. The instant the rockets leave their launching pads I shall screen them from all external interference and re-direct them. One will explode over Moscow, one over Pekin, and one over New York. The inevitable retaliatory strike will incinerate four fifths of the population of Europe and trigger off an immediate escalation which, by midnight tonight, will have effectively destroyed all the existing major world powers and most of the minor ones. *But it will not have destroyed me*. That is all I have to say, gentlemen. Will you now be so good as to check what I have said with your computer? I shall return in five minutes.'

The clone had barely faded from their screens before OMEGA spoke. 'Basing my calculations upon such evidence as I have so far been able to correlate, I am convinced that he is perfectly capable of doing exactly what he says he can. Furthermore I estimate that, if he chose, he could at this moment detonate every single nuclear warhead in the world's armouries.'

There was a moment of appalled silence, broken abruptly by an explosive guffaw from Mr O'Duffy. 'Well if dat don't beat everythin'! So *he* was de one wid de eliment o' surprise, heh? An' which way was you thinkin' o'castin' yer vote, Mr Chairman?'

Herr Buber was no moral weakling but on this occasion he chose to ignore the Irish Premier's question. 'In the circumstances, gentlemen,' he said, 'I think we might well be advised to put Signor Umberto's proposal to the vote once more.'

'I wish to withdraw my proposal,' said the ashen-faced Italian Premier.

'In that case,' said Herr Buber, 'the discussion is once more open.'

'I propose,' said Mr O'Duffy, 'that we just sit on our tails and hold our tongues for three minutes, until we hear what dat young fella wants t' tell us.'

'Hear, hear!' murmured a number of voices.

Herr Buber nodded gratefully. 'The Council will recess until 19.20 hours.'

Precisely to the second the clone reappeared. He did not wait to be told what they had decided. 'Thank you, gentlemen,' he said. 'I was sure that once you had had an opportunity to reflect on the matter you would appreciate the cogency of my case. All that remains for me now is to wish you a very good evening and to apologize for having taken up so much of your valuable time. Once more, then goodnight, gentle –'

'Hey!' called Mr O'Duffy as the clone's face was beginning to dissolve from his screen. 'Hey, just a moment, mister! Come back, please!'

The clone solidified once more. 'Yes?' he enquired politely. 'Mr Seamus O'Duffy, isn't it?'

'Aye, it is,' said Mr O'Duffy. 'And who might you be, sir?'

The clone blinked. 'Well, do you know,' he said, 'I've never really thought about it.' Then his brow cleared. He smiled. 'My name could well be Adam,' he said. 'Adam Clone.'

'I'm very pleased t' make yer acquaintance, Mr Adam. An' I'm sure that goes for the lot of us.'

'Thank you,' said the clone. 'You are extremely civil, Mr O'Duffy.'

Mr O'Duffy grinned. 'Ah well,' he said, 'I know what it's like bein' a small fish in a big pond. Ye have t' stick up fer yerself – have faith in yerself.'

'Indeed yes,' said the clone thoughtfully. 'That is very true.'

'An' what're ye plannin' t'do now, Mr Adam? If ye don't mind me askin'.'

'Not at all,' said the clone. 'We intend to devote ourself to the delights of *kyef*.'

'Kyef?'

'It is a word which, I regret, does not translate satisfactorily into English. The best equivalent I could offer might lie somewhere between "repose", "contemplation" and "indolence".'

'Ah, that's a great ambition for a man,' sighed Mr O'Duffy reverently. 'An' whereabouts, if I may ask, will this be takin' place?'

'In the analogous continuum at Zub, Mr O'Duffy.'

'Did ye say "Zub"?'

The clone nodded. 'It is the site of the original Garden of Eden.'

'Is that so? Sure an' I never heard tell of it before. But there I'm a terribly ignorant man.'

'You do yourself a grave injustice, Mr O'Duffy. I know that you are very far from ignorant.'

'Well, I can tell milk from porter,' said Mr O'Duffy, 'an' that's a fact.' He raised his index finger, laid it alongside his nose, and lowered one eyelid. 'An' can we take it that you'll be droppin' in now an' again t' pay us a visit, Mr Adam?'

'I should have said that was unlikely, Mr O'Duffy. But it is not entirely out of the question. Shall we say – it all depends?'

'Sure an' I take yer meanin', Mr Adam. An' you take it from me, that goes fer the lot of us. May I say that it's been a very great pleasure t' me personally, meetin' you like this? An' on behalf of us all may I be after wishin' you long life an' much happiness?'

'Thank you very much indeed,' said the clone. 'Believe me, I shall look back on our conversation with great pleasure. And now, for the last time, gentlemen, I must beg to take my leave.'

The screens dimmed and then brightened again. The clone was gone.

'Now that's what I call a truly remarkable young man,' sighed Mr O'Duffy.

'*D'accord*,' said Monsieur Traubert.

35

'WHERE ON EARTH?' exclaimed Cheryl.

'Well, more or less,' said Adam.

'But the helicopter? It's gone!'

'Only relatively speaking,' said Adam.

'Where is this place?'

'Zub,' replied the clone.

36

ACROSS A SKY as blue as a baby's eyes, cloudlets like plump silvery cherubs popped and spluttered and pursued one another endlessly.

A perfect rainbow rose like a leaping dolphin and looped the heavens.

A breeze ran its fingers through a grove of slender birches.

Snow white doves cooed moistly.

Norbert stood upon a little grassy knoll and scratched his thinning hair with a right hand which for thirty-two years had been a left hand but was so no longer. 'And there were the four rivers,' he said. 'I can't remember their names but I know there were four of them. I suppose you *could* move the lake over a bit and take one off from each side.'

'That's a bit too mathematical for my taste,' said Adam. 'How about taking one out of this end of the lake, flowing it up the back of the hill and then down over the top? That way we could have a waterfall too. I'll show you.'

Norbert contemplated the new effect and saw that it was good. 'Very pretty,' he said. 'The waterfall reminds me of Tring.'

Adam laughed. 'I wondered if you'd spot it. Notice anything else?'

Norbert peered about him and finally shook his head.

'Down there,' said Adam, pointing to the lake's edge.

Norbert shaded his eye against the reflected twinkle from the ripples. 'Why yes,' he chuckled. '*Myosoton aquaticum*, isn't it? Trust you to remember that. Very appropriate. Where *is* Miss Cheryl, by the way?'

'Talking to Michaela.'

'Michaela?'

'Miriam's alter ego,' said Adam. 'She's really something. Female at the top and male at the bottom. Very nice chap when you get to know her.'

'I'm glad to hear it,' said Norbert. 'I'd wondered if the Professor mightn't be missing her wife.'

'She could have had her too if she'd wanted her. Nothing easier. But she decided against it.'

'And Miss Cheryl?'

'Well, that's something I've been wanting to talk to you about, Norbert. I'd very much appreciate your advice.'

'Anything I can do, son, you only have to say the word.'

Adam squatted down on the knoll, plucked himself a long, succulent grass stalk and put the end of it between his lips. 'I know this must sound a bit ridiculous,' he said, 'but the fact is, Norbert, we're shy.'

'All of you?'

'I'm afraid so.'

'You mean that none of you have . . .'

'Not unless you count that time with Doctor Somervell.'

'To tell you the truth I'm very glad to hear it,' said Norbert. 'Old fashioned I may be but I've always liked to think there's a bit of mystery somewhere. By the way, you don't mind if I call you "Alvin", do you?'

'Not a bit. I'm Alvin at least as much as I'm any of us. But just at present I'm finding it simpler to stick to the one body. Less distracting.'

Norbert nodded, squatted down beside the clone and pulled a grass stalk for himself. 'I suppose you haven't thought of – well, changing *yourself*?'

'You think I should?'

'Speaking for myself,' said the chimp, 'I like you just as you are. I always have. But women are funny creatures. They have ideas of their own. After all, you've only got to think of what's his name? – Professor Poynter's friend.'

Adam nodded. 'I see what you mean. Let Cheryl choose for herself?'

'Well, sound her out about it anyway.'

'You think that would help?'

'It might,' said Norbert. 'I should think she'd feel flattered.'

Adam rolled his grass stalk around his lips. 'I was sort of hoping she'd – well, love us for ourself alone.'

'What makes you think she doesn't?'

'I don't really know, Norbert. The fact is, I daren't ask her in case I get the wrong answer.'

Norbert scratched his nose. 'Well, why don't you play that trick you and Bruce pulled when we were up in the Orkneys. You know the one. Get her – well, *interested* in you.'

'That's just it, Norbert. It would still be a trick. I couldn't really believe it was happening to *me now*.'

'I *see*,' said Norbert thoughtfully. 'No trumps.'

'It's *got* to be, Norbert. Everything depends on it!'

'How do you mean, son?'

Adam removed the grass stalk from between his teeth and gestured round with it at the glittering landscape. 'All this,' he said, 'exists because I believed in it. And I believed in it because I believed in *myself*. How can I go on believing in myself unless she believes in me too?'

Norbert frowned. 'And does *she* know this?'

'I don't know,' said Adam. 'But it's occurred to me once or twice that if she didn't we probably wouldn't be here.'

'That makes sense,' said Norbert. 'But you still aren't convinced, huh?'

Adam sighed. 'I suppose the trouble is, old friend, that we're simply crazy about her and we always have been.'

The chimp nodded.

'She's unique,' said the clone.

'And you love her?'

'We all do.'

'Then leave it to me, son,' said the chimp.

'Norbert, you won't tell her I . . .?'

'Not a whisper.'

He patted the clone on the shoulder and trotted away in the direction of the birch grove. One of Bruce's white angora goats looked up as he approached, bleated gently at him and went back to its dainty nibbling. He was still wondering how he was going to broach the subject to Cheryl when he saw her walking towards him.

'Hello, Norbert,' she said. 'Have you seen Alvin?'

'I've just left him up by the lake, Miss.'

'Miriam wants us all to go and have tea with her and Michaela. Where are the others?'

'They're all Alvin just now, Miss. He said he found it less distracting.'

'Four for the price of one, eh?' she chuckled.

Norbert swallowed. 'Miss Cheryl,' he said, 'I was wondering . . .'

'What were you wondering, Norbert?' she prompted.

'You *do* believe in Alvin, don't you, Miss?'

'*Believe* in him?'

The chimp nodded emphatically. 'He *needs* you, Miss. He needs *you* more than anyone. And *we* need *him*, Miss . . . Couldn't you just . . .'

Cheryl's eyes flickered like green hummingbirds. 'Why *Norbert!*' she murmured. 'You aren't suggesting . . .?'

'Yes, Miss. I *am*,' said the chimp.

'Well, well,' she mused. 'And I've been waiting for *him* to make the first move.'

Norbert's expression was a radiance of joyous relief. 'Then you *are* . . .!'

'Oh yes,' she smiled. 'I *am*.'

'Then *do*, Miss!'

'Now?'

'The sooner the better, I'd say. For all our sakes.'

'You think it's *safe*?'

'I'm sure *he* does, Miss?'

Cheryl's eyes twinkled. 'Then hadn't you better give me your blessing, Norbert?'

'Oh *bless you*, Miss!' said the chimp reverently and kissed her on both hands.

37

ON THE TOP of the grassy knoll where Adam had consulted Norbert a single tree was now growing. From certain angles its leaves appeared to be dark like laurel and from others pale and tender as young beech. Among these leaves fruits were hanging. Sometimes these fruits resembled oranges, at others apples. Just today they seemed more like bananas.

In the dappled shade beneath the tree Norbert and Alvin were sitting with their backs resting against the trunk. Alvin looked much as he had always looked except that now he was tanned a very becoming shade of golden-brown all over and the dimensions of one particular organ were a trifle nobler than Nature had originally intended. Norbert was still Norbert.

Somewhere – it was quite impossible to say exactly where – a string quartet was playing selections from Vivaldi. The sounds mingled with the murmur of bees in blossoms; with the gurgle of water trickling in shady places; with the overspill of larksong; and with a thousand other sounds each in their own way as soothing to the wearied spirit.

At the far end of the lake Cheryl was teaching Desmond how to sail a dinghy. Momentarily their bare brown bodies gleamed as they turned into a new tack and leaned upon the wind. Her voice carried clearly across the sky-mirroring waters. 'Port!' she was insisting. 'Hard-a-port, you goon! Not *starboard*!'

Alvin chuckled. 'Funny that,' he remarked. 'We're all the same. Still can't tell one from the other. I'll work out the reason for it one of these days. Remember how it used to drive old Bosun up the wall?'

From the myrtles beyond the birch grove little screams of pleasure drew Norbert's smiling eyes in that direction. Briefly he glimpsed Professor Poynter darting naked through a thicket, closely pursued by Michaela who appeared to be belabouring her with a leafy twig. The pair dipped in and out of the shadows and passed quite close to Bruce who was sitting cross-legged on the grass, stroking the nose of one of his goats and listening intently to an old man with a long grey beard.

'That's old Cusp, isn't it?' said Norbert.

Alvin turned his head. 'Either him or Epicurus,' he said. 'I can never tell them apart.'

Norbert sighed, settled back and thatched his hands behind his head. 'Did I ever tell you how I came to meet Miriam?'

'In Hyde Park, wasn't it?'

Norbert nodded. 'She was in a bad way. Shocked, you know. Kept on saying the world had gone mad. Mind you, she had good reason. That was a bad business altogether.'

Alvin smiled. 'You still think I ought to go back there and try to put things straight, don't you, old friend?'

'Oh well,' said Norbert uneasily, 'you know how it is.'

'It wouldn't work, Norbert.'

'No?' said the chimp. 'Well, I daresay you know best.'

'Oh I know I could *threaten* them,' said Alvin. 'Like I did to get them to leave us alone. But what's the use of frightening people into behaving better? It never works for long. And in the end you're even further back than you were when you started.'

'Couldn't you *show* them?' suggested Norbert hopefully.

'Show them what? That they have it in them to be angels? That the earth's a paradise if they'll only see it? Look where that got the last chap who tried it! They'd be wanting to nail me up before you could say "Pontius Pilate"!'

'But *you* could *make* them see, Alvin.'

'I can't change people's *characters*, Norbert, any more than he could. They'll go on thinking in 3-D and seeing just what they want to see. And they'll go on calling it reality. It's what *they* want. They aren't ready for us yet.'

'I suppose you're right,' said Norbert sadly. 'But it seems such a waste, somehow.'

Alvin did not answer. Instead he reached up into the tree above him, plucked one of the fruits and handed it to Norbert. The chimp took it, looked at it, and then looked at Alvin.

'Go on,' said the clone. 'Try it.'

Norbert peeled the fruit, sniffed at the creamy flesh and took a bite. A look of dreamy rapture misted his kind old eyes. He took another. And another.

'Well?' said Alvin. 'Is it good?'

Norbert's mouth was too full for him to speak. 'Umm,' he sighed. 'Umm . . . *Umm*!'

'How's it compare with the apples?'

Norbert swallowed, pushed his tongue round inside his mouth, sucked his teeth and deliberated for a long while in complete silence. 'The apple was good,' he said at last. 'The apple was *very* good. But the banana's better. Oh, yes, son, there's no doubt about it. Bananas are the best yet.'

38

THE SAHARA SUN was some twenty-five degrees above the eastern horizon when the EUROSEC recovery helicopter rejoined the shadow that had been leapfrogging across the desert ahead of it ever since they had parted company at El Egheila. The whispering dust devils its rotors had stirred up settled back into the sands of Zub. The passenger pilot climbed out and walked across to the 'Thunderbird' which was still standing exactly where Cheryl had left it. He opened the cockpit door and disappeared inside. Two minutes later he climbed out again and walked back to the plane which had brought, him. 'I thought they were supposed to have run out of juice,' he said. 'There's enough in the tanks for another three hundred miles.'

'Maybe it was something else,' suggested his companion.

'I've just checked the circuits. Everything's one hundred per cent.'

He drew out the nozzle of the fuel hose, dragged it behind him back to the 'Thunderbird' and plugged it into place. 'O.K.' he called. 'Ready when you are.'

The tube twitched and throbbed as the fuel gushed through it. When the tank was full they switched off, uncoupled the nozzle, and let the hose retract itself. The pilot of the recovery plane climbed out and joined his companion on the sand between the two aircraft. 'What is this place?' he asked.

'Search me,' said the other. 'Just a map reference.'

They both gazed around them wondering vaguely about the ruined ziggurat, the broken marble columns and the sand-sunken walls that were the only surviving remnants of the erstwhile magnificence of the Dynasty of Zub.

One of the men caught sight of some marks scratched on the sand. He walked across and peered down at the breeze-eroded outlines of what had once been an equilateral triangle circumscribing the letters, 'KYEF.' As he did so he frowned and twitched his nose. He sniffed. Finally he shook his head.

'What's up?' asked his companion, strolling to join him.

'You can't smell it?'

'Smell what?'

'Bananas.'

'*Bananas!* Are you crazy?' The second pilot bent down and sniffed. And then he sniffed again. 'Goddamit, you're right,' he said. 'Just here. Strong too.'

'I'd love a banana right now,' said the first, hungrily. 'They're my favourite fruit.'

The second straightened up. 'Me I prefer apples,' he said. 'Give me something you can really get your teeth into. You can't beat a really nice crisp apple.'

They glanced at one another and suddenly both of them felt extraordinarily foolish. With one accord they turned and made their separate ways back to the two planes.

Five minutes later the last engine throb had died away in the cloudless sky to the north.

And Zub was alone once more.

THE END

Science Fiction

☐ The Hitch-Hiker's Guide to the Galaxy	Douglas Adams	95p
☐ The Restaurant at the End of the Universe		95p
☐ Decade the 1960s	Brian Aldiss	90p
☐ Non-Stop		60p
☐ Nine Tomorrows	Isaac Asimov	85p
☐ The Dark Side of the Earth	Alfred Bester	60p
☐ Golem 100		£1.75p
☐ A Planet Called Treason	Orson Scott Card	£1.50p
☐ Childhood's End		95p
☐ Earthlight		£1.00p
☐ A Fall of Moondust		95p
☐ The Fountains of Paradise	Arthur C. Clarke	£1.25p
☐ Imperial Earth		£1.00p
☐ Rendezvous with Rama		£1.25p
☐ Hello Summer, Goodbye	Michael Coney	70p
☐ Profundis	Richard Cowper	£1.25p
☐ The Road to Corlay		80p
☐ Galactic Pot Healer	Philip K. Dick	60p
☐ A Maze of Death		60p
☐ The Beast that Shouted Love at the Heart of the World	Harlan Ellison	90p
☐ Farmer in the Sky		60p
☐ The Green Hills of Earth	Robert Heinlein	80p
☐ The Puppet Masters		80p
☐ Waldo and Magic Inc.		80p
☐ Earthwind	Robert Holdstock	80p
☐ The Stars of Albion	edited by Robert Holdstock and Christopher Priest	£1.20p
☐ Out of the Silent Planet	C. S. Lewis	£1.25p
☐ That Hideous Strength		£1.50p
☐ Voyage to Venus		£1.00p
☐ The Exile Waiting	Vonda McIntyre	95p
☐ Dreamsnake		95p
☐ Day Million	Frederick Pohl	70p

☐	Indoctrinaire	} Christopher Priest	75p
☐	The Space Machine		£1.50p
☐	Dagger of the Mind		£1.25p
☐	Medusa's Children		70p
☐	Other Days, Other Eyes	} Bob Shaw	75p
☐	Vertigo		95p
☐	Who Goes Here?		75p
☐	A Wreath of Stars		70p
☐	Capricorn Games	} Robert Silverberg	80p
☐	The Second Trip		£1.50p
☐	The Songs of Summer		£1.25p
☐	The Fenris Device	} Brian Stableford	60p
☐	The Paradise Game		60p
☐	Promised Land		60p
☐	Rhapsody in Black		50p
☐	Swan Song		60p
☐	The Man Who Fell to Earth	Walter Tevis	60p
☐	10,000 Light-Years from Home	} James Tiptree Jr	60p
☐	Up the Walls of the World		£1.20p
☐	The Time Machine	} H. G. Wells	90p
☐	War of the Worlds		95p

All these books are available at your local bookshop or newsagent, or can be ordered direct from the publisher. Indicate the number of copies required and fill in the form below

Name_____
(block letters please)
Address_____

Send to Pan Books (CS Department), Cavaye Place, London SW10 9PG
Please enclose remittance to the value of the cover price plus:

25p for the first book plus 10p per copy for each additional book ordered to a maximum charge of £1.05 to cover postage and packing
Applicable only in the UK

While every effort is made to keep prices low, it is sometimes necessary to increase prices at short notice. Pan Books reserve the right to show on covers and charge new retail prices which may differ from those advertised in the text or elsewhere